DE SADE'S VALET

The publishers gratefully acknowledge the kind assistance received from the following organizations towards the publication of this book:

The European Commission Ariane Programme

Norla (Norwegian Literature Abroad) and the Norwegian Embassy in London

The Arts Council of England

DE SADE'S VALET

A *novel by*
Nikolaj Frobenius

Translated from the Norwegian
by Tom Geddes

MARION BOYARS
LONDON • NEW YORK

First published in Great Britain and the United States in 2000 by
MARION BOYARS PUBLISHERS
24 Lacy Road, London SW15 1NL
1489 Lincoln Avenue, Saint Paul MN55105

Originally published in 1996 by Gyldendal Norsk Forlag A/S
under the title *Latours katalog*.

www.marionboyars.co.uk

Distributed in Australia and New Zealand by Peribo Pty Ltd,
58 Beamount Road, Kuring-gai, NSW 2080

Printed in 2000
10 9 8 7 6 5 4 3

© Gyldendal Norsk Forlag A/S 1996
© This translation Tom Geddes 2000

The right of Nikolaj Frobenius and Tom Geddes to be identified as
authors of this work has been asserted by them in accordance with the
Copyright, Designs and Patents Act 1988.

A CIP catalogue record for this book is available from the British Library.

A CIP catalog record for this book is available from the Library of Congress.

ISBN 0-7145-3060-3 Paperback

Typeset by Ann Buchan (Typesetters), Middlesex
Printed and bound in Great Britain by The Bath Press, Bath

The publishers would like to dedicate this book
to the memory of Joan Tate, translator and tireless
promoter of Scandinavian culture,
who died 6 June 2000.

1

The Moneylender's Son

Once upon a time, many years ago, there lived in the little harbour town of Honfleur, on the coast of Normandy, a woman who was extremely ugly. So ugly was she that passers-by halted in the street to look at her. At her forehead, her blue-veined face, her tufted warts and her bull neck. She was a woman of gigantic proportions, and people declared that she was twice her natural size. She was so gross that many found it hard to believe what they saw. This creature seemed to bear little resemblance to a human being: she was deformed, night-marish. In the opinion of travellers she was the most repulsive woman in the whole of France, and the local market-women whispered that she was an emissary of the Underworld, a woman with the face of the Devil. Did she also dream the Devil's dreams? Her appearance was so striking that everyone stopped and stared at her, as if dazzled by her beauty. They could not avert their gaze, could not turn and go on their way. They stared and stared until their eyes ached. At an impossible vision, a masterpiece of ugliness. The woman with this power of attraction was called Bou-Bou Quiros, and her previous history was a singular one.

France under Louis XIV was a land of plenty. Truffles, lavender water, pride, war, debts, smallpox. Even infants abandoned on church steps, bawling in a fury that seemed to come from time immemorial: you fiends, don't leave me here all alone! That was how Bou-Bou's life began. She was on her own. Starving. Her prospects limited to a frugal childhood in a convent with the nuns, work as a wet-nurse or in the paper mill, a few painful childbirths and a premature demise from bubonic plague or dysentery. Let us be generous and give her forty years in the stinking industrial city of Rouen, and a pauper's grave: a simple cross with her initials carved upon it. That was the inevitable future for a fat, ugly orphan girl born in 1728. But no — fortune was destined to smile on her. Unlikely as it might seem. Why just on her? For the nuns and the other orphaned children the events were startling and shook them to the roots of their being, implying as they did that life was unpredictable and that the future might hold even greater surprises.

It so happened that a well-to-do but childless couple came walking along the path by the convent and caught sight of a girl in the long grass between the cultivated beds of the garden. The woman stopped, approached the fence and gazed upon Bou-Bou's dirty face. As soon as she realized the woman was peering at her, Bou-Bou began to cry. She was sure she must have done something wrong again, even if she did not know what, and that the woman was about to scold her. Thinking it best to forestall punishment, she opened the floodgates. The woman went up closer to the fence to see why the girl was crying. She was the wife of Dr Quiros, thirty years old and regarded by her husband as having a decidedly sentimental disposition. She stood there leaning over the low fence and was immediately moved by the child's distress. All at once she felt as if she were weightless, as if she were falling, sucked into a whirlpool. She had suffered such attacks quite often recently and had learnt to remain outwardly composed, even if her mind was in turmoil. This time it was different. When she opened her eyes again, she saw the little girl's fear as a sign. She recognized in the unattractive face her own despair and was suffused by a feeling of warmth. Everything would change now. She would take the child under her wing. She climbed over the fence, raised her aloft and marched off towards the entrance to the convent.

Love. She would use that word without embarrassment or self-doubt whenever she spoke of Bou-Bou. She devoted all her time to the little girl from the convent. Bou-Bou was washed clean with kisses, her shapeless body wrapped in silken cloth. The toneless monosyllables she emitted were met with enraptured smiles, and Bou-Bou was soon transformed into joy incarnate. She frolicked in the woods, plucked flowers in the meadows and squinted up at the sun.

For a surgeon, Dr Quiros had had a remarkable career. He was a short, stout man. His thick, stubby fingers looked totally unsuited to the finer tasks of medicine. Yet even as a little boy, when adults had asked him what he wanted to be in life, he would put on an intransigent expression and almost spit out the word 'do'tor'. He seemed absolutely determined on it, and his unwavering insistence was such that his parents allowed him to accompany his uncle on his journeys to the market-places, where quacks and sawbones demonstrated their skills. An inventive man, his uncle had concocted a popular animal oil which he claimed was distilled from ox-horn. This *oleum animale* was reputed to extend human life by a century or two. His uncle himself died at the age of sixty-one.

So young Quiros travelled around with his uncle to the markets of northern France and studied the skills of the surgeons with rapt attention. He later became a specialist in bladder-stone surgery, which in those days was an excruciatingly agonizing procedure. On a study trip to England he witnessed an operation at St Thomas's Hospital in which the surgeon removed the 'stone' in less than sixty seconds. Amazing. This new 'lateral surgery' meant that Quiros was able to operate on ten times as many patients and increase his wealth substantially. People came to him from all over Normandy to put an end to their torment. Dr Quiros could pick and choose his patients and he was not shy about taking a generous fee. The gardener and the maids had to have their wages, after all; his wife needed her clothes from Paris, and Bou-Bou her own governess. The fact that Bou-Bou had developed so monstrous a form despite the meagre fare provided by the nuns was a phenomenon the doctor ascribed to the wonders of God's creation rather than to metabolism. When his anxious wife asked him about their child's size and diet, he responded with airy phrases about the manifold variety of nature. Were fish and elephants not different, and tigers and chickens? His wife nodded pensively. He told Bou-Bou later on that human beings were created inherently good. But if anyone made insulting remarks about her, she should pretend not to have heard. Thus everything was arranged for the benefit of the child. She learnt to sew and to dance and how to behave in polite society. She tasted truffles from Périgord. The governess had orders to mould her mind in the spirit of the Enlightenment. Their adopted daughter should learn to read, write and count as if she were a boy. Bou-Bou was good at arithmetic and read both Montesquieu and Racine. She became an educated young lady. Her parents' love had made her forget what she had once been. And her father had great plans for her. She would be his business assistant, helping her old father in his mission of removing all bladder stones from this world.

But is life not cruel? Why should all this be taken from her? Why should she be granted a taste of happiness if it was only to be snatched away, leaving nothing but bitter yearning in her heart?

Bou-Bou was fourteen. She stood amid the ashes of the fire that had consumed her parents' home, holding a metal casket in her hands. 'God has taken everything from me,' she thought. 'And worst of all, He has let me survive, as if He needed a witness. And He has given me this casket, so that I may live and never be allowed to forget. It must be a test. Because if I don't manage to go on living, He will know they are right, the people who have always said that my body is Satan's work and that I have the Devil's seed in my heart.' Bou-Bou looked down at the casket and knew that this legacy from her parents was the very thing that had made it possible for them to adopt her and turn her life into something more than meaningless obscurity: Money. She decided then and there to devote her life to its pursuit.

She left Rouen and bought herself a little cottage in the hills above the harbour town of Honfleur. Apple trees. A verdant valley. Boats on a blue-black sea. It all seemed to her incredibly beautiful. She was still only a child but so corpulent that everyone assumed her to be a grown woman. Monsieur Goupils, an ambitious lawyer, himself a hunchback, had received her in the office of his recently deceased father. His eyes lit up when she opened the casket of gold coins. There was enough there, let me see — his avaricious brain made a swift calculation — there was enough in the casket to buy a house in one of the better districts of Paris. But he knew that was just another dream.

'I want a simple house that I can live in for the rest of my life. I have to save my money, you see, to make sure that I can get by.'

The girl's sombre voice brought Goupils back to the provincial business affairs of Honfleur. Where were the ideals, the visions, that would change the world? He straightened up as much as he could and offered her the only property he had available, a hovel that had stood empty for a year since the death of its owner and which, despite the absurdly low price, no one wanted to buy. It was rumoured that wild beasts had taken up residence there.

'This could be exactly what you're looking for, Mademoiselle,' said Goupils.

Bou-Bou came to like the cottage. It was a simple stone dwelling high above the town. You could see the whole of Honfleur and the Seine estuary from the window. To the east the hillside was covered with overgrown apple orchards, and in the spring she could stand in the back garden and look out over an ocean of white blossom. It was an hour's walk down twisting paths to the town, but Bou-Bou preferred to do that than to give the apple-pickers the pleasure of laughing at her behind her back whenever she bought a pail of fruit. She could consume the sweet apples in great quantities. Avidly. The taste of them reminded her of her adoptive mother and of the orchard at home. She never seemed able to satisfy the hunger that left her stomach always craving for more.

The loneliness did not bother her. But the silence did. She had never lived anywhere so quiet. When she awoke in the mornings she was surrounded by it, like an invisible force; she felt it was akin to death. It lay upon her like a heavy coat, paralyzing her. She would sit gazing out of the window like an old woman. Clouds of pollen. The incessant motion of the sea. Animals at the edge of the wood, glinting in the sunlight. She was convinced that sooner or later someone would emerge from those woods. And one day, after an endless succession of days when nothing happened, a man did indeed appear, in a dark cloak and silken knee-breeches: it was Monsieur Goupils. Bou-Bou was disappointed.

'I've been thinking about you, Mademoiselle, and wondering how you were getting on.'

His voice was high-pitched and reminded her of one of the ancient nuns at the convent. He looked about him with scarcely concealed curiosity. At the bare walls. At the dish of apples. At the big loaf she had just baked. Bou-Bou did not know what to say.

'I'm happy here in my cottage.'

Was that a stupid thing to have said? She followed his gaze back to the bare walls. He squared his shoulders to the best of his ability and looked at her face, at her body, at her breasts and belly with no sign of shame or embarrassment. Was there a gleam in his eye? Was it contempt or inquisitiveness? His breathing quickened.

'We could do business, Bou-Bou, you and I. Business that would give you security. You have a lot of money lying around in the house. You're all alone. Somebody might find out about it — and that would not be good for you.'

Bou-Bou lowered her eyes. She would rather not let him see that she was angered by his half-veiled threat. But he changed his tone, and she looked up at him again.

'Times are hard, Bou-Bou. Farmers, fishermen, boatbuilders are all trying to borrow money. Why not lend out yours? To people who need it. And get three times as much in return.'

He had a broad grin on his face, obviously pleased with himself. Bou-Bou felt the urge to grin back at him, because she liked talking about money, but she knew that would be a tactical error. Instead she pouted, as if assessing his intentions. Yet she could not suppress a smile as she asked, 'And your commission, Monsieur?'

Goupils drew up his head a little, clearly disconcerted.

'Bou-Bou, I'm a modest man. And in your case I would make a virtue of my modest requirements. Just ten per cent of the amount of the loan, plus thirty-five per cent of your annual earnings. What do you say to that, my dear?'

She gave a short, caustic laugh and was pleased with the sound. This lawyer must think her more of an idiot than she was, but he was the one who was making such a blatant fool of himself. She enjoyed watching him show himself up and shook her head slowly, the way her adoptive father had done whenever he wanted to emphasize anything.

'Ten per cent of the amount on repayment of the loan, and not a sou more. And if you don't wish to do business on those terms, I'm sure I can find another lawyer who will. That is my final offer, Monsieur.'

And so it came about that Bou-Bou Quiros began her unscrupulous and lucrative career as a moneylender in Honfleur and its environs. A necessary evil was how people described her business and called her the Devil's own pawnbroker on earth. Again the Devil's name was invoked in connection with her. But she remained indifferent to such remarks.

Her life had taken a new direction. Suddenly she had enough to do. Promissory notes covered the table. Loan agreements. Interest payments. Signatures. Payment schedules. Profit figures. She and Goupils often sat long into the night going over the accounts. And the silence bothered her no more. She took a strange delight in the thought of all the money she was making. She was not worried about her borrowers; their need was no concern of hers. Bou-Bou had always felt herself isolated from the world around her, and her debtors' misery was an aphrodisiac: earning money gave her a glow of satisfaction. She had become a moneylender because God had decided she should go on living, or simply because she enjoyed it. The whole thing was too good to be true. She loved the thought that her capital was being doubled. Quintupled. Multiplied tenfold. Drawing up the weekly accounts thrilled her. Precise calculations. Assessments of outstanding loans. Insistence on the fulfilment of every condition. It was her profession.

'Merciless.'

'Heartless.'

These were some of the mutterings of her clients.

'Masterly,' thought Goupils, but he had the sense to play the part of an independent intermediary. For Bou-Bou, her activities had the straightforward clarity of an arithmetical equation. It never occurred to her that sympathy should be any part of it. She was quite unruffled by the fact that people felt exploited by landowners, envied the men of the church and hated bloodsuckers and moneylenders such as her. Life was unjust, people starved, there was nothing she could do about it. Perhaps legitimate profit necessarily involved a little injustice. Why should she let it bother her? On the other hand she was quite moderate in financial matters: she never raised her interest rates, did not cheat with promissory notes and took no more than the moneylenders of Rouen or Lisieux. She demanded what she thought looked reasonable for the accounts.

Her dreams were about money. About numbers. About promissory notes. About gold coins. Money had an intense fascination for her, as if she were a collector. She loved coins for their own sake and never gave much thought to potential uses for her fortune.

Then an odd thing happened. As her activities developed into a daily routine, her body began to breathe in a way she considered unseemly. It was as if the coins, promissory notes and accounts exerted a secret power over her and made her flesh awaken like an animal from hibernation. Her skin felt the caress of her clothes, became sensitive to chance contact. Every time she touched anyone, whether it was in the queues at the market stalls or in a dry handshake from Goupils, a quiver ran through her that was almost painful. In bed her breasts moved like independent beings, pointed their nipples in the air, rubbed against each other. The behaviour of her thighs, posterior and groin was even more indecent. Eventually she had to pleasure herself in order to get to sleep. Filled with shame, she cried out her desire. And tried to ignore it. But it continued to torment her. Like an itch.

*

The man wending his way through the trees had been a fugitive for so long that the only end he could see before him was death. He had five days' growth of beard, and his bare feet were black with dried blood. The look of an escaped prisoner was imprinted on his features. He did not dare venture into the harbour town, and all his plans and energy had evaporated. His greatest desire was simply to lie down on the mossy ground and sink into oblivion. He was not afraid at the thought of death: he would much rather die than end up back in a dank cell. But he lacked the courage to die. He shut his eyes and trudged on, heedless of the branches striking him in the face.

When he realized that he had emerged from the wood, he opened his eyes and stood still. At the top of the slope ahead of him there was a stone cottage with a deserted air. A half-open door. A dark window. He looked about him, conscious only that he had been walking all through the night. He approached cautiously. He could hear no sound and the nearer he came, the more convinced he was that the house was empty. He pushed open the door and stepped into the darkness. The room seemed to close in on him before he became aware of the smell of food. How could he not have noticed it before? It was certainly strong enough. He had to laugh. As a convict it had been five years since he had last tasted roast meat, and now he could no longer recognize it; yet he had always known whether the warders were bringing gruel or soup, and whether there was a strip of pork fat in it, long before it even reached the corridor to the cells. He had been too preoccupied with listening to identify the aroma that was now tickling his nostrils. He stood motionless in the dark and knew it was too late to retreat; this was a smell he could never turn his back on. He moved warily towards the kitchen table. He found the dish of meat just by sniffing: chunks of succulent beef, fried in good butter and seasoned with parsley. He began to eat voraciously, mouthfuls so huge that he had difficulty in getting them down. 'I'm eating like a hog,' he thought, 'I'm worse than the wild beasts I've been wandering among for the last five days.' But he couldn't stop himself: he ate until he had to double over and vomit on the floor, and it was as much as he could do to resist picking out the biggest pieces to swallow again.

Then the first bright rays of the spring sun slanted in through the window and shone on him as he knelt there on the floor over his own vomit. And at that very same moment he heard the sound of a sleeping woman. There was no doubt at all in his mind that it was a woman, and he could see from the things in the kitchen that she lived alone. He stood up and listened. Wiped his mouth. The sound of a sleeping woman. He closed his eyes and pictured her. He climbed the stairs to the bedroom on tiptoe. He could already feel desire burning in his loins. His hands were shaking so much that he was hardly able to open the door.

The blanket was suddenly stripped away, and a hot wind seemed to blow into her. She put up no opposition, clinging to the unknown insistent presence. Her womb swelled and she was filled with fluid. The pain made her go hot and cold and forced from her an involuntary gasp in a voice she did not recognize as her own. As the stranger slumped down on her body and gave a sigh of satisfaction, she trembled with lust, not with fear. In the silence that followed she lay dozing, suffused all at once with a feeling of happiness. Nor did she show any interest whatsoever in the stranger when he began to talk and talk, telling her about prisons and crimes as if he believed his outpouring of words could lighten the darkness and change everything. The only thing she could see was a girl in the beech woods, eleven years old, wearing a dress with ruched sleeves. The girl was sauntering through the trees and came to a clearing, where she sat down on a tree stump and pulled her skirt up over her thighs, letting the spring sun bathe her private parts in its warmth. With this image of herself in her mind, Bou-Bou fell asleep, while the man at her side continued his incessant talk. Time went backwards in her dream, her adoptive parents turned into the nuns at the convent, and finally she was lying on the church steps wrapped in a blanket.

She woke up with a shriek. Peered frantically about the room. There was no longer a man at her side. Just a few black hairs on the bedclothes, in the hollow where he had lain. She got up and scrubbed the sheets. Aired the room. Cleaned it from top to bottom. For the first few days after the shock she felt numb, afraid he might return. But when nothing happened her unease gave way to a feeling of warm contentment in her belly. She tried to think what the man had talked about and what he was called. She could remember hearing a name, but was not sure whether it was his or just a chance word in the flow of speech. The name was Latour.

*

She was screaming so loud in the pain of her labour that the dust flew up from the floor, screams so intolerable that the midwife had to stuff a shoe in her mouth to make her desist.

At last the little bundle was pulled out and deposited in the embrace of its weeping mother. Wriggling and squirming, the baby opened his eyes and stared at her searchingly. It struck Bou-Bou that the eyes had a roguish glint. It was as if the boy were assessing her, to find out who had given birth to him and what sort of world he had come into. Bou-Bou kissed his sticky face and gazed in enchantment at his sea-blue eyes, his crooked little nose and the black down on his head. She loved him already. Then he started yelling at the top of his voice.

The midwife came in with a bowl of water and took up the new-born infant in her arms. He gave her a kick as he was removed from his mother, as if he already understood that he could not expect anything good from anyone other than her. With practised movements the midwife washed him clean of slime and blood. She raised her eyebrows as she examined the creature. He was very small to have come out of Bou-Bou. His face was absolutely round and chinless, his skin puckered like that of an old man. His nose looked as if it were broken, and he had a projecting upper jaw that gave him the appearance of a rodent. 'He's an ugly child, there's no doubt about it,' the midwife thought to herself, 'but it's not to be wondered at.' She held the struggling baby tight and rinsed the blood out of his sparse black hair. She washed him thoroughly, and with every wipe of the cloth more of him became visible. The more she saw of him, the more nervous she became. She had seen many unprepossessing babies in her time, but this little boy was quite simply . . . as ugly as the Devil. She stared into his hideous little face as she wiped the cloth over his head. The boy opened his tiny mouth and *hissed*. In alarm and fright she let him drop into the bowl of water and stepped back a few paces. It was a hiss so venomous that it sent a cold shiver right through her. Bou-Bou was already sitting up in bed and shouting at her to remove him from the bowl. Her cry was so sharp and aggressive that the midwife momentarily forgot her abject horror and went over and picked him up. Bou-Bou gave her a look that seemed to threaten some awful violence if anything of the sort should happen again. The midwife held the baby away from her body with trembling hands. She did not want to be near it, did not want to have to look at it. But being inquisitive by nature, even though she had closed her eyes in fear of the Devil and intended to keep them closed until she was well outside the house, she opened one eye now just a fraction to take a peep at the little rascal. He was staring straight at her. At first with something resembling the pent-up anger and hatred of a grown man, then with a shift of countenance that gradually became a beaming smile. His eyes twinkled at her most engagingly, sea-blue and penetrating. In amazement she opened both her eyes. She found it difficult to believe that the boy was trying to ingratiate himself with her, but that was how it seemed. Her trembling abated. Strange, she thought, his eyes are actually . . . beautiful, quite beautiful. They didn't go with the ugly face, they seemed to be totally distinct from the dreadful child himself. She couldn't help it: she returned his smile and gave him a cautious hug. Bou-Bou, having now risen from her blood-soaked mattress, went up to her and grabbed the child to herself with an aggrieved expression. The midwife was taken aback, and slowly started collecting her things together. She left the cottage under Bou-Bou's disapproving gaze. It was only later, as she was walking along the Rue St Léonard, past the boatbuilders, heading for her own house on the outskirts of town, that she recalled the baby's appearance and the hiss he had emitted and once again she felt a cold shiver of fear.

She told everyone she knew that Bou-Bou had given birth to a son, and the gossip on the street spread like wildfire through the town. The whole of Honfleur soon knew about the terrible child with the sea-blue eyes, and people began to mutter about *malificarum* and the ways of the Devil. Even the priest became apprehensive. The only one to ignore the rumours was Goupils. He was convinced it was all lies and slander, and went to visit Bou-Bou a few days later.

He came to the house partly to talk business and partly to be able to dismiss the speculation once and for all. He found everything in good order. Bou-Bou was happy, and the boy looked completely normal, even though Goupils had to admit that he had never seen an uglier child. Seeking further assurance of the absurdity of the townspeople's talk, he stroked the baby's head. The boy cooed as all babies do. There was nothing especially menacing about him. Goupils smiled inwardly, thinking disdainfully how easily frightened people were. They would snap at anything and consume it greedily, making no use of the faculty of reason that nature had endowed them with as human beings. He kissed Bou-Bou on both cheeks and congratulated her. Then he bent down to kiss the baby. But, looking into those cold blue eyes, he too was gripped by a feeling of unease and made haste to leave the house.

It was some while before Bou-Bou observed that the boy could feel no pain. She found out the first time she went to trim his nails. His baby nails were difficult to snip with big scissors, and, despite taking the utmost care she inadvertently cut his finger and made it bleed. She immediately said she was sorry and oohed and aahed, but Latour just stared up at her uncomprehendingly. He regarded his bleeding finger with no change of demeanour. Bou-Bou was astonished. Did babies not know they were supposed to cry in pain without being told to by their parents? She cast her mind back to her own childhood but all she could remember was that she was afraid of being hurt. She tried to reassure herself that the boy would start screaming soon enough but also thought that if he did not feel anything, it could only be to his advantage.

When Bou-Bou first took him into Honfleur, people crowded round her in eager yet timorous curiosity. Bou-Bou, overcome by her confused feelings of mother-love and assuming they had come to admire her beautiful child, showed him off proudly. The market women looked upon him with such veneration that Bou-Bou was put in mind of the infant Jesus. They peered at his little face and as quickly drew back again. Bou-Bou laughed and told them about everything a baby does, things that seem wonderful to a mother but are quite ordinary and even tedious for everyone else. Her anecdotes aroused little interest among the women and they soon departed. It was not the spawn of the Devil, anyway, they thought. Idle gossip. Admittedly he was too ugly for words, quite obnoxious in fact, but there was something about him that mitigated their contempt, something in his deep blue eyes that engendered a sort of . . . respect. For there was no gainsaying, even if they had wanted to, that Latour-Martin Quiros, as the boy was later to be christened, had eyes like those of the children in the portraits of that great painter, Greuze. They were beautiful, and seemed to have a soothing effect on others. Every time Bou-Bou took him to Honfleur, people came up to her to stare at his little face as if to reassure themselves that he really did have a frightful visage. And yet a pair of eyes that bore witness to the compassion of God.

When the priest rather unwillingly scooped water over the boy's head from the font in the church and muttered his blessings, he kicked out and hit him right on the chin. The priest lurched backwards with the child in his arms. With an anxious and pained expression he handed him over to his mother again. On the way home Bou-Bou began to feel worried. She had stopped on the church steps and clipped the boy's ear and scolded him for kicking the priest, but Latour had just gazed up at her serenely. Even if she pinched him hard until she got cramp in her fingers he did not react. As she took the short cut through the woods towards her cottage, she realized that she had no idea of what she should do as a mother, how she should bring him up, admonish him or show him both love and discipline. What was a mother to do with a child who could feel no pain?

*

Bou-Bou had thought herself surrounded by reflections. She had seen herself in puddles, in the water-tank, in a shiny apple. Or rather, she had seen her belly. Everything had reflected the unborn: the whole of creation was pregnant. She could imagine she had become twice as big as before and, for the first time, had been proud of her size; it was proof that the child was thriving. In reality she had not grown that much bigger than normal, but the roundness of her belly had shifted, taken on a different form, become firmer. Every night she had sat up naked in bed with her eyes focussed resolutely on her navel. It was as if she could see it expanding. And then came the sounds. Butterfly sounds. Rumbling. Drumming. In the end the little rogue had beat his fists against the membrane of his universe with all his might. He had struck harder and harder, and it echoed like music in the room, or so it seemed to her. She had been afraid. She had cowered under the blankets and tried to escape the conviction that she was unfit to be a mother and that she would do the world and the child a service by killing it as soon as she could. Such thoughts had come like waves of pain but were interspersed with more positive feelings, even sparks of optimism. She had strode off down to the market in Honfleur and bought octopus, something she usually never ate. She devoured as much of it as she could get, raw octopus, grilled octopus, octopus soup. It was still not enough. The whole house smelt of octopus. When Goupils came on his weekly visits he had to hold a handkerchief up to his nose. But despite her eccentric behaviour and glowing face, nobody had guessed that Bou-Bou Quiros was pregnant. Her body appeared outwardly unchanged, and the joy she radiated was seen as shameless arrogance. The bloodsucker was even happy, and had the gall to show it!

She had not been concerned about the whispers or the looks of hatred while she was pregnant but, now that she had the child, she found people's enmity threatening and seldom left the house. Nursing the child was like a love ritual: she lay with him at her side on the bed and let him go to sleep with milk in his mouth. Her nipples were sore from his ardour, and her womb was still bleeding and painful from the birth. But the blissful joy of maternal love lightened her troubles. Bou-Bou had never dreamt that she would be a mother; such a notion would have been beyond her imagination. She thus felt herself blessed and was giddy with pride. Whenever her little boy awoke in the night with a whimper or a cough, she was horrified and momentarily convinced he was going to die. It was as if she had been presented with a gift intended for a member of the nobility and was afraid someone would discover the mistake and come and take it back.

She wept whenever she found she could not pacify the baby and thought herself incapable of caring for him. She lived in perpetual dread of incompetence and infanticide. She would lock the door of his room and hide at the other end of the cottage. She would crawl into a corner of the kitchen, or run out into the woods where she could be alone. It often took her hours before she could calm herself sufficiently to dare go back in to him. By then his bedclothes would be wet with tears and vomit. Bou-Bou would punish herself by not eating for a whole day. Her most fervent wish was to be a good mother to Latour. She wanted to give him a love that was greater than herself.

Latour would sit playing contentedly under the table. From the earliest age he exhibited the greatest dexterity and took special delight in small intricate objects. He caught two grasshoppers and by holding their back legs and wings gently against their bodies he was able to snap off their four front legs. That left them distinctly unbalanced and no longer able to hop or fly. They dragged themselves around in semi-circles, leaving trails of green slime behind them on the stone floor, as if all the colour were draining out of them. Latour sat motionless, following the beautiful creatures with his eyes and listening to their anguished chirping. He sat there in absolute silence and concentration, watching their contortions. His child's face lit up when they gathered their strength and made a desperate leap with their hind legs, buzzed their wings and fell back in the same position with their heads on the floor and their feelers like two outstretched arms in front of them. Then his expression changed, and his eyes filled with some kind of sympathy. He got right down on a level with the grasshoppers' eyes, but they looked lifeless. He tapped them on their rears, and they made another attempt to stagger forward. Latour smiled again in gratification.

Then he would crawl out from under the table, very slowly, as if not to anticipate his joy. He looked up at his mother's face, giggling uncontrollably. When she put down her account books or chopping board and lifted him up, he would close his eyes and press his nose into the odours of sweat and olive oil between her enormous breasts. A sea of comfort. He kissed her profusely. On the occasions when his mother locked herself in her bedroom, he would tug at the handle in vain. He knew she was in there, but she would not answer, so he would stand for ages at the door listening. It was so quiet that he could almost imagine she had gone away. Then when she came out again, he would embrace her so passionately that she felt ashamed.

In the eyes of others Bou-Bou was a usurer, a whore of repayments with interest, vulgar and avaricious. But the quietness that permeated the house and made everything echo with exaggerated noise — pots and pans, the jingling of coins, the scraping of pen on promissory notes — provided an environment in which it would take a long time for Latour to realize that his mother was anything other than a sea of comfort.

When mother and son went into town hand in hand, the women scowled at them from the doorways in the Rue du Puit. They hissed and spat at them. Bou-Bou pretended not to see or hear, but the boy stared back at them, and the openness of his gaze made them unsure of themselves and silenced them. Speculation was rife, however. Mademoiselle Quiros had deserved to give birth to a pig, but there was clearly something special about this boy. Who was the father? Bou-Bou had never been seen near a man, of course. She had lived alone in that little hovel for four years, and it was unthinkable that any of the young lads of the town would have roamed around up there and paid court to her. Had a blind man come out of the woods? Had Bou-Bou mated with a goat, or a stallion? A sailor so hungry for female flesh that he had not seen what he lay with? The old crones whispered that it must have been the Devil himself who had crept between her thighs, to spread his depravity over the earth. But since no one had seen anything, and nothing could be proved, the rumours died away, and they all decided to ignore the whole affair and pretend the boy did not exist. But it was a decision difficult to adhere to, because the little boy appeared to hold a particular fascination for the townswomen. They cast covert glances at him and crowded round him in the less frequented back streets. They examined him avidly and made excuses to touch his lined and wrinkled face. They giggled and asked him all sorts of questions. One morning the priest's sister came upon three young women with Latour by the salt warehouses.

'Keep away from him! Keep away! Can't you see there's the Devil in him, the serpent, the roaring lion?'

She pointed a trembling finger at Latour, and the girls scrutinized his face more carefully. They noted his receding jaw, his skin, his melancholy expression and large cold eyes and were once again suffused with a rapturous shudder. They turned to the priest's sister and shook their heads in unison. She was a neurotic old bag of bones.

'Hussies! Do you want to end up in a pit of fire and brimstone? Can't you see he's playing games with you already?'

Then she embarked on a long lecture about sin and temptation.

'I shall get my brother to take up the matter,' she concluded and hastened away. After this incident the women of Honfleur were more careful about going right up to him. And every Sunday the priest, under pressure from his sister, warned the congregation against letting curiosity and desire prevail over virtue, reason and faith. But the women continued to watch Latour in secret and contrived to go near him while pretending they were on other business.

*

So now, on the rare occasions when Bou-Bou left the cottage, the cottage with the soft shadows, the cottage that had become an extension of her own body, of her limbs and flesh and smell, and waddled down the path to go to the market, the townswomen turned their backs on her. Their fear and hatred of her

29

and the attention her appearance provoked had been transformed into indifference by the birth of Latour. It was as if Bou-Bou had been forgotten by Honfleur and gradually she seemed to forget Honfleur too. There were never any decent people in the town anyway, just itinerant vendors, sailors who got drunk at the inn and not a soul who had ever had a kind word for her. Only the man who had come to her that night — and Latour. She had got used to Honfleur and forgotten her anxiety that she would never make a good mother. She read in a book a sentence she liked so much that she could sit and read it again and again: 'Then she experienced equilibrium in her life.' Equilibrium. It had a ring of dignity and distance, and she told herself that that was what she was experiencing. Equilibrium in her life. She became obsessed by the word and by the idea that she was living a harmonious existence. Yet, despite this new-found harmony, her old frustration would still surface, like a ghost from the past. She tried to convince herself that these were just intermittent aberrations. She was in a state of equilibrium, after all. Every time her frustration drove her out of the house, behind locked doors or into dark corners, she felt a sense of failure. Afterwards she would get angry and completely lose her temper, hurling things at the boy in a violent rage. Only at nightfall would she pick the book up again and lie down and read that soothing sentence by the light of a flickering lamp.

It was several years before Bou-Bou finally admitted that Latour had an evil side to his character. She patiently tried talking him into better ways, having imbibed her adoptive parents' views that everyone was created good by nature. But Latour was a wicked child. He put on theatrical productions with partially dismembered insects under the dead apple tree in the garden. He loved going down to the orchard to watch the butterflies and moths as they swarmed to lay their eggs in the apple blossom. He shouted out words of encouragement to the beautiful clouds of leaf-roller moths, to the great annoyance of the fruit farmer, who was vainly attempting to destroy them as pests. After dark he would run about, throwing stones up at the stars. 'Next time I'll get one!'

He chased the cat all over the house, and one morning Bou-Bou found it hanging in a tree. Latour unequivocally denied having anything to do with it, claiming that some youths had been skulking round the house at dusk, and he seemed to believe it himself. Bou-Bou knew he was lying but she merely told him, yet again, that hurting animals was wrong and that he shouldn't do it. If she scolded him with enough love in her voice, he would surely come to recognize the difference between good and evil in the end, she thought, forcing herself to forget his misdeeds.

Latour simply smiled and gazed straight through her with a far-away look in his eyes. He would sometimes burst into laughter at her moralizing sermons. He could easily have feigned the sentiments that were apparently expected and yet were so alien to him, but he already found them ridiculous and meaningless. Why should he feel remorse? He had killed a cat. So what? The cat killed birds. Birds ate insects. Why should he pretend to be filled with remorse? He could not understand Bou-Bou's concern.

A strange sensation of power and pleasure crept over him every time he held a tiny creature in his hands and wondered what to do with it. The insect or animal would lie there before him, unable to move. Latour experienced a profound tranquillity. He would sit immobile, and actually sense the pain flowing through the little creature. There was an icy tingle in his chest. A lightness in his head. A dull twinge in his stomach. It was like a trance. He was in a state of ecstasy. Sometimes he felt this ritual as a kind of release. When the creature finally died, he would close his eyes. He felt a momentary sadness, then relief.

He was aware that he did not feel pain like other people. He looked at his mother's face in astonishment whenever she cut herself or had aches and pains in her body. She often got blisters on her feet, and he liked to sit and bathe them for her and apply ointment while watching her agonized expression with detached curiosity.

Perhaps he had a need to experience the pain of others, Bou-Bou thought to herself, trying to ignore the uneasy feeling his inquisitive look instilled in her.

He was an imaginative child and played at being the bandits from her bedtime stories with such enthusiasm that he terrified her, dressing up in dark cloaks and speaking in disguised voices. To see how long her patience would last. It was apparently infinite. But Latour suspected there must be some limit and had decided to try and find it. What would she do when she could tolerate no more of his behaviour? Would she hit him even though she knew it did not hurt? Would she punish him by withholding food from him, though she knew only too well that he just became debilitated and did not feel hunger the way others did? What would she do? Latour teased, tormented and threatened. He was adept at finding her weak spots and knew exactly what to do to annoy her. But Bou-Bou kept her self-control. When he finally found her limit he was shocked by her reaction. Bou-Bou simply stopped talking to him. She behaved as if he were not there. That was the punishment: she pretended he did not exist. It was far more unpleasant than he could ever have imagined and too much for him to bear. He padded around behind her making abject conciliatory noises and offering to do any number of jobs for her. But Bou-Bou's face was like a mask. Latour got no sleep until the punishment came to an end and he vowed that he would torment her no more. But Bou-Bou was no longer so patient anyway. From time to time her rage would erupt, and the kitchen would be reduced to ruins, and he would have no idea why. Then she would not speak to him for several days again. Latour inured himself to her silence towards him. He sat listening to her dark mutterings in the kitchen and looked out at the sea and sky, unable to compose his thoughts. He was like a blank canvas, a brush stroke not yet applied. Only when his mother forgave him and they were reconciled did he feel himself once more a whole person.

'There's nothing I lack,' said Bou-Bou to herself. 'Things couldn't be better.' Her life was in a state of equilibrium. For the first time she felt fulfilled and contented. But as soon as the thought occurred to her, she was afraid. She remembered that just once before she had felt completely happy and without a care in the world and immediately afterwards had been left standing in the ashes of everything she had possessed. So when her business affairs began to run into difficulties she found it a comparative consolation. One farmer was digging his heels in and refusing to pay his interest. Goupils and Bou-Bou had several evening meetings. She was suddenly in need of his support, his resourcefulness, his contacts. Bou-Bou herself was in favour of overlooking this one failure to pay but she could see the overwhelming logic of Goupils' argument: if they let one person get away without paying, in the end no one would pay. Goupils quietly got in touch with an unemployed blacksmith and two farmhands from Lisieux. And they quietly broke the farmer's kneecaps one night, and people quietly carried on paying their interest, with injured expressions on their faces.

Late one evening Goupils brought a pistol to the cottage. He had heard rumours, rumours of some petty villains with evil intent, and it was best to be on the safe side. Bou-Bou thanked him, surprised by his sudden concern. It was the first time she had thanked him for anything, and his boyish smile embarrassed her.

And sure enough one night two angry youths turned up at Bou-Bou's house.

'That damned moneylender is taking the very food out of our mouths!'

They had been drinking cider and were brandishing their knives in the air, each trying to outshout the other.

'Let's get in there and make mincemeat of her!'

The alcohol fuelled their loathing, and they kicked down the door and ran up the stairs with their knives at the ready. But Bou-Bou was standing by her bed with the pistol in her hand. She screamed at the first boy who came at her. An unambiguous roar. When he did not stop but just hurtled towards her like a sack through the air with his knife raised, she shot him through the head. A perfect shot. He was thrown back and fell on his friend who was still climbing the stairs. Bou-Bou was convinced that her life and her child's were at stake, so she rushed down the stairs after them and pointed the pistol at the young man who was lying quaking with fear beneath the body of his companion.

'Jesus . . . Mary . . . Mother of God . . . Save me . . .'

Bou-Bou loaded a new bullet into the gun and killed him with a shot to the chest.

Latour stood at the top of the stairs, trembling. He was sure it must have been Bou-Bou's scream he had heard, and that she was dead. His little body was shaking all over, and it made no difference when his mother came running back up the stairs and hugged him to her. For several minutes he was certain she was dead, and not even her body against his could convince him otherwise. In these few motherless moments the walls and roof caved in on him and everything went black. Long afterwards he would still brood on that sudden darkness that had enveloped him. And when it came back to him in a dream, one night in Paris many years later, he would wake up shrieking in fear. Realizing now that his mother was still alive — he was by then lying with his head in the crook of her arm and listening to the comforting murmur of her voice — he had a great desire to see the dead men.

As she slept, he extricated himself from her embrace and crept down the stairs. The two youths lay half on top of each other, as if they had fallen in a scuffle and could not get up again. He descended cautiously and bent over their unmoving faces. They were both tall, with pale eyes and reddish blond hair. They could have been brothers, thought Latour, crouching down to look into their eyes. He had heard that you should close the eyes of the dead, so that they could leave the earth and see into eternity. Did that mean that the dead could still see, he wondered, and was that why their eyes looked so sad? He closed the eyelids of the youth lying uppermost, and then reached across his stomach to do the same for the one who had been shot first, now half covered by his brother. His face was besmirched with blood. Latour was just about to put his fingers on his eyelids when the boy turned his head from one side to the other and attempted to focus his blurred vision. He was alive. Latour remained motionless. The boy opened his mouth in an attempt to say something but could not form the words. Latour lay on the stairs, watching his face for a long time. It was quite still. Perhaps it was the pain that kept him so still. Latour wished he could feel some of the pain and thought that then they might be able to be friends. When finally the boy managed to speak, Latour was not listening. It was too late. A smile crossed Latour's features, and in that same instant the boy closed his eyes. After a while Latour realized he was dead. Yet he went on lying there gazing at their pale, peaceful faces, and experienced the same feeling of relief as when he saw a grasshopper disappear into the undergrowth.

This episode did not make Bou-Bou any more popular in Honfleur. But it restored respect for both her and Goupils. Their co-operation entered a new phase. Goupils gave up his role as independent agent, and Bou-Bou allowed him thirty-five per cent of the takings. They were the evil twins of Honfleur and they raked in money by the sackful. Goupils came to the cottage more and more frequently, sometimes sitting long into the night discussing rates of interest and the financial soundness of borrowers. And Bou-Bou discovered that she liked having him there, liked the gentlemanly attention he paid her and his talent for figures. In the end, to her own great surprise, she found herself looking forward to his visits. She began putting on make-up, combing her hair, powdering her cheeks. Even though the break-in and the 'manslaughter in self-defence' (in the laconic police phraseology) had not changed Bou-Bou's life, she had become more apprehensive. She persuaded Goupils that they should lower their interest rates, and he readily agreed when he perceived it would improve their relations with the townsfolk.

Goupils was quick to broadcast the news. 'We have the lowest interest rates in the whole of Normandy,' he boasted at the inn. But the ropemakers and the tannery owners and the local shipbuilders were not impressed. It stank of bribery. To think that their goodwill could be bought for blood-money was an insult. People talked of going to the more expensive moneylenders in Lisieux, as a matter of principle and pride. And, although most continued to go to Goupils' office to pay their interest, there were many who paid off their accounts and stopped coming. Poor folks' pride. It came as a blow to Goupils, but he knew that he should have expected it. From now on he would spend less time in town and more at Bou-

Bou's cottage. That was where the future and the money were, he thought, and could not deny that he often hankered after the extensive creature comforts she had to offer. Whether he was attracted by money or by love he had no idea, and saw no reason to ask himself awkward questions.

For Bou-Bou this new animosity from the people of Honfleur meant nothing at all. She was certain that the reduction in interest rates had taken the sting out of the hatred towards her, and anyway it was not intended as a gesture of goodwill. Her judgement was to prove right. No more unwanted guests visited her at night: she could sleep soundly again. With Latour in his own bedroom, she finally plucked up courage and invited Goupils to stay the night. She enjoyed the sight of his boyish smile between her breasts, and his panting sighs made her feel fulfilled.

For Latour one thing was absolutely clear. Goupils was the cause of his mother not caring about him any longer. Bou-Bou must have become totally mixed up in her feelings. She was flattered by the fact that Goupils was sniffing around her like a lovesick dog, and it was impossible to talk to her. Latour was sure his mother would only get angry if he tried to point out Goupils' obvious defects: he was greedy, cowardly, dishonest and hypocritical, to name but a few, and he was also mean and small-minded. But were he to say anything to her, she would think he was trying to destroy her new life. That would be dangerous.

He lay awake all night worrying about the best way to proceed, listening to the noises of their repulsive lovemaking filtering through the wall from the next room. He thought of Goupils' happy face. And of ways of killing him. Until he had worked himself almost into a frenzy with the plethora of ideas. Should he poison the verminous reptile or set a deadly ambush for him? He could climb up into a tree by the path and drop a sizeable rock on his head as he passed underneath on his horse, the mare that he had laughingly called Bou after Latour's mother. He could drag the lawyer's corpse up to the cottage and tell his mother in tears that Goupils had fallen from the top of the hill. An accident. He screwed up his eyes and tried to think of something that would get him to sleep. By daybreak his feeling of repugnance was so intense that sheer exhaustion finally overcame him.

When he awoke he had decided on a plan. While Goupils was still asleep in Bou-Bou's arms he crept out of the house with a spade. By the steep stony hillside where the path turned off to Honfleur he dug a deep pit and covered it with branches and leaves. Then he climbed a nearby tree and settled down to wait. Sitting in the tree with the salty morning breeze off the sea in his face, heavy-limbed after only a few hours' repose, it was as if he were watching the path below him from a star up in the heavens. Everything seemed so remote, even the tree he was clinging to. His arms looked like some other boy's, not like his own at all. It was somehow a comforting thought. He was not filled with hatred any longer, and as he stared down at the path and imagined what was soon to happen, his mind was quite clear. Goupils always rode this way to Honfleur and used to tell Bou-Bou about his ride. This morning he would get a surprise. Bou would round the bend and fall into the pit and Goupils would be thrown off the horse and down the hill. Latour would be above him in the tree silently witnessing his struggle for life. He started planning what he would do next and what story he would tell his mother.

But when Goupils came riding out of the wood towards the steep drop at the edge of the path Latour saw that his plot was not going to go as intended. Goupils was riding too slowly. The mare was ambling along, and Goupils seemed in no hurry. He was smiling, and his whole face radiated relaxed contentment. Latour ground his forehead against the tree trunk. He felt the muscles tightening in his chest and came over giddy. As the mare stepped into the foliage and slid down into the hole with Goupils on her back, and the sharp rocks positively glistened with their absence of torn flesh, Latour was so aghast that he lost his grip on the tree-trunk and tumbled through the branches, cursing as he fell. Goupils emerged without a scratch and strode calmly over to him. Latour saw the toes of the lawyer's boots and closed his eyes to wait for the kicks. But nothing happened. Goupils went back to the hole, drew his pistol, took aim and shot the whinnying horse. Returning to Latour, he ordered him back to the cottage. As they walked in silence Latour tried to convince himself that Goupils would beat him, that he would think, 'I'll teach the boy to feel pain.' He had no fear of the stick. What he feared, and could not bear to contemplate, was how many days would elapse before his mother would speak to him again.

Goupils took him into the garden and tied him to an apple tree with the harness. Then he went on into the cottage, and Latour could hear their voices, but not what they were saying. Goupils and his mother were talking in a low undertone. Latour consoled himself with the thought that the punishment would come soon, and that Goupils would hit him so hard that he would feel pain, and that his mother would forgive him when she saw how much he was hurt. But many hours passed without anything happening. Latour stood lashed to the apple tree all day, all evening and all night. He listened to the indistinct voices from inside the house and could see a weak glow from the lamp, and in the end there was nothing he wanted more than for someone to come and beat him. But it was not until the next day that Goupils came out to the garden and released him. Latour sank to his knees before him. He wept and begged to be punished. But Goupils just went on his way. A few days later he came riding back on a mare that was exactly like the one he had shot. And she was also called Bou.

*

'What is pain?'

Latour thought there were four different types of pain. Everyday pain. Deep-rooted pain. The pain that came from heart and stomach. And the pain that came from thinking too much. He never ceased to be amazed at the grimaces on Bou-Bou's face whenever she had sore blisters. He felt nothing himself, and sometimes wondered whether he was fully alive. Deep-rooted pain was totally unintelligible to him. You could fight against it, he thought, but then it just seemed to become worse. Or you could surrender to it and embrace it. The mental pain that Latour had felt when Goupils tied him to the tree in the garden and made him wait there for a punishment that never materialized was for him a false and unpleasant pain. It was impossible to control and made him wish he were dead. Now he could no longer look Goupils in the eye without remembering that the lawyer had in effect made a contract with him from which it was impossible to withdraw. He had settled matters with Latour without punishing him, and so Latour was bound to an unrequited need for punishment and a pain he could only dream of. That made Goupils all-powerful and plunged Latour into misery. He also felt another kind of mental pain when he sat in the woods pondering Honfleur and the townswomen and the inexplicable loathing in the eyes of people who did not even know him. The power of the priest and Goupils' machinations: this was the pain you feel when you know you are enslaved by something you do not understand.

Even though he still lived in the midst of all the cooking smells of the kitchen, in the midst of Bou-Bou's and Goupils' business affairs and inflated expressions of love, he was thinking that really it was all gone. It had become the past. He kept away from the cottage now. He played with the daughters of the fruit farmer, Regnault. They were delightful with their rounded bellies and each with a birthmark on her nose. He enticed them into his secret lair, a den he had built in the woods. The two girls were enchanted by the tales he told about the Forest King, a mighty being who could make magical things happen to them if they would just show themselves naked to him. Latour presided over events in a knowledgeable manner, making sure that everything was done in accordance with the Forest King's wishes. The two delicate little girls stood in the hut of leaves and branches without a stitch on them, trembling with cold and excitement, while Latour circled round them, narrowing his eyes, scratching his head: that was not enough, the Forest King was not pleased, they were to lie on their backs and lift their legs in the air, as high as they could, so that His Majesty could see them properly. The girls looked askance at one another, but the expression on Latour's face convinced them, and they did as he instructed. His curiosity was satisfied, and he was able to tell them in a quavering voice that the Forest King was content. What a strange invention a girl's body was. He went home to Bou-Bou, and for once laid his head on her arm.

He took up a new hobby. The apple orchards and green meadows above Honfleur made the area attractive to butter-flies. They fluttered around the flowers, thistles and thyme, and Latour had always been fascinated by them. They provided a glittering shimmer of blue, a flash of scarlet, bewitching flecks of colour in the green of the foliage. He learnt their names and practised identifying them. The admiral, its wings velvety black with white speckles and orange stripes; the reddish brown peacock with a violet 'eye' on each wing. Colourful tortoiseshells, swallowtails, purple emperors. Lemon yellow and dark green, bright blue and white. He hunted out the most brilliant species and liked to watch them as they settled in the trees and on the underside of leaves. Their elegant flight through the air sent a shiver of joy up his spine, but when they disappeared over the tree tops, and he did not know whether he would see them again, he was so overcome with desire that he started catching them. At first he released them after a while but then he discovered that he could kill them and dry them and they would always retain their beauty. He kept them in a box in the outhouse and took them out at intervals, pretending they were alive again and flying gracefully above his head. He used the outhouse as a workshop and preferred spending his time with his butterfly collection to having to listen to Goupils' nonsensical chatter.

One day Bou-Bou told Latour he would have to attend the Catholic primary school in Honfleur. The proposal immediately aroused his resistance: he did not want to sit with the other boys in Honfleur being instructed by the priest. Bou-Bou had to force him to go.

Latour was aware of the inimical expressions on the faces of his fellow-pupils and listened to Father Martin's monotonous prayers in horror. He had no reason to expect that either the teacher or the pupils would be particularly friendly towards him. Father Martin was strict and demanded impeccable behaviour. It was possible to win his approval in some measure by employing polite language and good deportment. He was temperamental and quick to anger at his pupils' lack of education. They had to show respect and humility towards teacher, church, religion and their fellows. Education was an end in itself. His cane was hard, and he struck hard if he felt that his formal principles were not being observed. Latour coped better with this regime than he expected. He paid attention to his teacher and liked his stern face.

Outside lessons Latour overheard odd words, phrases, whispered comments. All concerning his mother. The boys showed him a new side of her, as if he were being introduced to a twin he did not know she had, a twin who was shameless and avaricious. She took the food from the mouths of little children and let the poor die of hunger, all for her own profit. They measured him with glances that seemed to say, 'We know who you are and we know we're not going to have anything to do with you because you're the son of the moneylender.' They called him the snake. The nickname was repeated everywhere he went, on the square in front of the church, in the classroom, a faint, almost inaudible sibilance. Even the wind, the streams, the trees whispered it, or so it seemed to him; it was as if the whole of nature had turned against him and despised him. One day four boys tried to drown him by the harbour. They covered him with stones and ran away when they thought he was dead. He regarded them with amazement but gradually became infused with hatred towards them and promised himself revenge. He always played alone and did not impose himself on the others. Their contempt for him made him feel stronger and superior to them. He knew they were not capable of forming an opinion of their own; they had been told who he was and that they should not go near him and they obeyed blindly, like sheep. He wept in secret when he could find no way of taking his revenge.

He sat with his back to them, his eyes firmly fixed on Father Martin, and felt like one of the last of the knights. The world was full of hostility, but he would not let himself succumb to this plague that had so ravaged the human race. He must fight against it and rise above his enemies. But this approach bore no fruit; it seemed to have no effect at all on the other boys.

He gradually began to look them in the face and decided he would let it be clearly written on his countenance that he was Latour, the well-behaved, considerate and obliging Latour. It was no easy undertaking. It was such a strain being nice. But the deception worked. The eyes of the sheep took on a more human expression, and when they opened their mouths sounds issued forth that occasionally even resembled sensible discourse. Latour felt sufficiently secure now to embark on minor acts of vengeance: petty thefts and untruthful stories. The square in front of the church was an excellent site for laying his traps. He was never found out and started actually enjoying school. Perhaps the world was not as cruel as he had at first thought. And he had learnt something in Father Martin's classes: that hypocrisy was the key to success and that life in general was so constructed that you could get away with the most evil deeds as long as you carried them out with style.

Bou-Bou had adopted the habit of reading. Now that she had become well-to-do, and thought herself above the common rabble, she wanted Latour to have an education befitting his position. He would not be like the fishermen's children in Honfleur. This accorded perfectly with Father Martin's educational precepts. She obtained the books of La Salle and Callière on etiquette and various other tomes on education. On polite conversation and table manners, on propriety between men and women, on bodily hygiene and suitable attire. Latour learnt that it was unseemly to drink soup from the bowl, to pick up meat with your fingers, to put bread in your mouth while holding a knife in your hand. Wiping your nose was a tricky subject, and Latour was given thorough guidance on what was acceptable. Bou-Bou taught him with authoritative voice.

'You must always use a handkerchief to wipe your nose and

try to turn your head away. Make no noise, Latour, people who do that have no idea what education is. Don't take too long getting your handkerchief out, because that shows a lack of respect, and when you've wiped your nose, don't look into the cloth to see how much of it you've used, whatever you do! Fold it quickly and put it back in your pocket.'

Latour nodded vigorously to indicate his pious regard for Bou-Bou's injunctions. Since she now spent a lot of time talking to travelling booksellers, she was soon persuaded that the boy also needed educative stories, on virtue and valour, warning the young against dissolute living and guiding them along the right path. She positively threw herself into moral tales, and Latour was enjoined to read them the moment she had turned the last page. They were soon sitting in their chairs engrossed in their books and forgetting to eat. The only difference was that whereas Bou-Bou wept at the virtuous girls' defilement, dishonour or tragic end, Latour admired the unscrupulous libertines, rogues and swindlers. For him their exploits were manifestations of their strong will, trickery was resistance, defilement hope.

At school, Father Martin started giving them lectures on anatomy. It was one of his favourite subjects. He gave a thorough introduction to the six branches of anatomy, waxing lyrical about bone structure and joints, muscles and brain. Latour thought he could discern a genuine sparkle in his teacher's eyes. Anatomy was expounded to them as a journey into the inside of the human body. With the aid of a doll he showed them how so many of the important discoveries had been made. Some of the boys were alarmed by his intensity, but Latour was unable to get the subject out of his mind.

He was one of Father Martin's best pupils. He was especially good at French and Latin. He had no trouble at all in reading extracts from Cicero and from Phaedrus' *Fables*. In

History, he made a good impression with his memory for dates. He liked Geography. But whenever Father Martin turned to theology and morals, Latour's eyes glazed over.

Father Martin was angered by Latour's vacant air and lack of concentration in these classes and punished him with fifteen strokes of the cane. It did not hurt him, but the expressions of the other boys filled him with fear: there was malice and vengefulness in their eyes. So from then on he always pretended to be listening.

Father Martin was also a man who believed implicitly in his own theory that good conduct was the solution to all problems and he had no sympathy for the animosity towards Latour merely because he was the moneylender's son. He even praised him for his good manners. It was thus quite natural that one day he should take Latour aside at the end of the last lesson and ask him if he would run a short errand for him.

'Of course, Monsieur.'

'My uncle Léopold lives in a little hut east of Regnault's orchard. I have a package for him. Could you take it to him this afternoon? He's a frail old man with rather idiosyncratic interests. Just call him Monsieur Léopold and simply say "no thank you" if he should happen to invite you in, which I don't think he will. Will you do that for me?'

Latour bowed his assent and took the package. It was wrapped in thick brown paper tied with string, and Father Martin had written his uncle's name in neat letters on the front. It emitted a strong, sweet smell.

Monsieur Léopold's hut was not visible from the path, and had he not had his wits about him, Latour would have gone past the tiny track that led off to it. He pushed through the undergrowth and came to a small yard with tools and wooden crates lying around all over the place. He stopped; it was raining, his face was dripping with water, and his lips were wet. The green-painted hut looked as if it had grown into the surrounding foliage, he thought. It was so strange that the uncle of Father Martin should be a man who received mysterious packages and lived in a hut in the woods. There was a seagull standing on the step in front of the door with its beak in the air, staring straight at him, as if wondering what he was doing there. Its wings were extended out from its body. Wasn't it going to fly away? No, it was absolutely still, as if waiting for something. Latour moved closer, very tentatively. The bird just went on staring at him. He crept forward a few more paces. And now he could see that it was perched on a wooden board, its gaze no longer on him but fixed straight ahead, over the tops of the trees. Latour had never seen a stuffed bird before. He sat down on the step and studied the dead gull at close quarters. He inspected the brownish grey stripes down the length of the feathers and the little red spot on the underside of the beak. Holding the bird up in the rain, he ran his finger over the reddish grey feet that were glued to the wood. He looked into the gull's eyes. Staring. Cold. Yet somehow alive. It was as if it had frozen stiff just as it was about to take off.

Then he heard something. A knocking sound. He held the package tight against his chest and went up to the door, waiting until the noise stopped. He rapped on the door, like an echo. There was a moment's silence before a voice shouted from within.

'Don't stand there banging on the door! Come on in!'

He remembered Father Martin's warning not to go into his uncle's hut; but it felt impossible not to obey.

'Come in!'

He opened the door and stepped hesitantly inside. There was a bitter smell in the air. He looked round cautiously in the light from the window. In the middle of the room was a man sitting at a big workbench facing away from him. Beyond him he caught a glimpse of a kitchen alcove with a wood-burning stove, a bedroom and rows of bookshelves. The bench was covered in knives, pliers, clamps and pieces of wood, a few bird corpses and an animal that resembled an enormous golden dog. *What on earth could it be?* The man at the bench turned round and peered in Latour's direction.

'Ah!'

He grabbed a silver-headed stick and came across the room at some speed. Latour backed up against the wall. The unknown man frightened him: could this really be Father Martin's uncle? His white wig hung from his head in one immense tangle, the skin of his face was wrinkled and his clothes were covered in white powder. Yet there was an air of refinement about him. His eyes lit up when he saw the parcel Latour was holding in his hands.

'Tobacco!'

Latour stared at him in incomprehension. Was it really tobacco? Could he smoke as much as that?

'Don't stand there like an imbecile, boy. Take it to the table and unwrap it carefully.'

He was already out of the door. Latour went obediently over to the bench and put the parcel down. He could hear the man rummaging around outside. And the soft patter of the rain in the trees. He looked at the instruments: knives, strange pincers. The paws of the golden dog hung over the edge of the workbench. It was unbelievably large, he thought, and had black stripes in its coat. Could there be dogs like that in Honfleur? With the utmost care he began to untie the string and open up the wrapping paper.

Monsieur Léopold came striding back into the room behind him with a tub under his arm, and, unable to restrain himself any longer, Latour turned and said, 'Excuse me for asking, Monsieur Léopold, but where did you get this dog?'

Léopold gave him a brusque glance, then his face creased into a grimace, and he began to smile.

'It's not a dog, my little innocent, it's an Indian cat, and it's called a tiger. There you are, you've learnt something today that you won't forget. Am I right?'

Latour nodded.

'Good. Let's get the tobacco unwrapped — we've got important work ahead of us.'

Latour cleared his throat and stammered, 'But Father Martin said I was not to . . .'

'This is an historic event, my boy. And I'm pleased that chance, as in all great moments of history, has decided to play its part by sending me an assistant. The first tiger ever to be stuffed in Normandy, by Léopold-Alphonse-Philippe Martin. The great master. So, let's make a start. We have important work to do.'

Latour inspected the tiger in front of him. He could smell the odour of decay and found it both sweet and pungent, reminiscent of his mother's breath in the mornings.

The tiger had been caught by the captain of a Navy vessel at harbour in the Gulf of Cambay. It was a ten-foot-long short-haired male, a Bengal tiger, *Felis tigris*, with the broad head and light beard that tigers of a certain age acquire. The captain had been so delighted at having caught something so exotic that he put it in a cage in the hold to ship home. But the tiger injured itself on the voyage and when the ship arrived at Cherbourg it had to be put down. The captain had asked for it to be stuffed so that he could keep it himself as a trophy. Léopold, who had an unblemished reputation as an anatomist and surgeon after twenty years in Paris and extensive experience as a taxidermist, was recommended by a collector in Le Havre, despite his age and eccentricity. He was the best in the area, perhaps in the whole of France, it was said. Léopold had taken on the commission enthusiastically, immediately putting all other work aside. It was a wonderful animal, and even though one paw was badly damaged, he was convinced that the captain would be pleased with the result. A solution of salt and spirit had been prepared, and he had ordered tobacco and tansy through his nephew for the actual stuffing.

He put a rope round the tiger's neck and tied it to a hook on the ceiling. Its upper torso was lifted slightly above the bench as if it were suspended in mid-air. Latour gazed at the beautiful creature, this magnificent cat, with its enormous tongue lolling out of its mouth, and tried to suppress his own feeling of nausea. Was he to help 'stuff' this? Léopold was washing his hands in a basin and humming a tune, while at the same time casting brief glances across at the tiger as if challenging it to battle. Outside the rain was falling harder. Latour thought it was odd that someone could stuff animals as a profession.

Léopold asked him to pass the biggest knife from the table under the window. It had a dark wooden handle, and the long blade gleamed. As Latour handed it to him he knew he could not leave now, and that he must try to throw off his squeamishness. He folded his arms and assumed an unconcerned expression, pretending to himself that he was Léopold's favourite nephew, treated with special consideration by the old man.

Léopold slid the blade expertly into the golden body. He made one incision from throat to anus and another from one front leg across to the other. Layers of pink flesh came into sight beneath the fur, opening up to reveal the most remarkable internal organs. Latour stared in fascination at the skinning process, his face screwed up in horror, but unable to look away, not wanting to miss anything. It felt good to be a favourite nephew and be here with the expert, learning all there was to know about techniques and animals' bodies and the use of instruments, while outside the rain was pouring down and all the other children were either bored or fetching water for their mothers.

One paw was removed from its joint, the tail was pulled out, and as Léopold peeled off the skin with a practised hand the bones and sinews of the hind part of the animal came into view. He had stopped humming and was concentrating fully now. From time to time he checked that Latour was following his every move. The skin was gradually coming away from the mass of bloody flesh that had flopped back on to the bench top. The smell of the corpse was strong, but Latour told himself he did not mind strong smells, in fact he rather liked them.

The master stood over the tiger with an air of satisfaction. The first bout between himself and the corpse had been won. Latour's feeling of nausea had vanished. The flaying, with its gory and apparently chaotic results, no longer troubled him. As cut by cut the tiger became less of a tiger and more of a solid red mass, his initial feelings of empathy with the animal disappeared, and he was curious to see how it could be turned into something more lifelike. They carried the pelt over to a tub at one end of the room and dipped it in the solution of salt and spirit and burnt alum. It sank to the bottom of the tub and absorbed the liquid rapidly. Léopold lifted the body on to a cloth and made ready to start the most complicated aspect of the whole procedure, the skinning of the head.

Latour washed the blood off the bench. Léopold had come to a pause in his preparations. He was standing very stiff and upright, with one eye closed, his head on one side in its tousled wig, thinking — thinking perhaps of the tiger in the wild, hearing its roar, seeing it bound across the plains. Latour stood as still as Monsieur Léopold, imagining himself one day imitating, and surpassing, the old man's flawless technique. Finally Léopold shook his head and emerged from his reverie. He looked at Latour and sighed contentedly. 'He is happy,' thought

Latour. Before them lay the corpse of the tiger. Thin streams of red fluid were leaking from the neck, stomach and feet. Latour felt a spasm of nausea again and looked out of the window. The rain was still falling on the trees, shadows were creeping over the path, the gulls were screeching from afar, and everything was quite ordinary, totally untouched by what was happening in the hut.

'Give the table a good scrub, my boy, we haven't got time to stand here dreaming!'

Latour obeyed without giving a thought to any alternative. He soon had the bench clean again.

The tiger's head had been severed at the vertebral atlas. That was the only way to do it. If the head were left attached to the body, there would be problems later with the musculature of the chin, Léopold explained, watching Latour closely. Latour thought his eyes shone as bright as the sun.

'Gently does it, now.'

Latour handed him a small knife and the master began the incision into the neck. The knife came up over the skull and down between the eyes. He stopped there, put the knife to one side and inserted his fingers carefully under the skin, moving them further and further round. Slowly the skin came away from the eye sockets. It was important not to let any of the fur be torn from the skin. He used the knife to cut away a strip of blue flesh against the eyeball on either side, and with that the skin came free. It dropped down over the face, exposing the eyeballs.

'At last!'

Latour stared from the tiger to Léopold and back again. The dead animal had lost its face. It was no more than meat and fat and cavities. Just a general shape. The thought struck him that in fact everyone looked like that. Under their fine skin even the abbot and the priest's wife were no more than gaping cavities and dark flesh; behind the sweetly innocent faces of the Regnault sisters the same dark shape lay hidden. Father Martin was a skeleton of bones with a mass of sinews and organs under the surface. Léopold's dexterous handling of the knife brought him back to the dissection on the bench. The lips were being cut away, the point of the knife slid round the base of the nose, and then Latour was staring into the tiger's mouth. Léopold's hands were working very slowly, in complete control.

Lips, nose, eyes, eyelids were all removed and put aside.

The skull was simmered over gentle heat for an hour.

'That saves us work. The cavities will be clean and free from fat.'

Léopold sat down in an armchair to smoke a clay pipe. It was the first time Latour had seen him relax. He inhaled the smoke deep into his lungs, and Latour waited for it to come out again from between his lips, but nothing happened: the smoke had disappeared into his body.

'Isn't he a magnificent beast? Isn't he amazing?'

His green eyes were sizing up Latour, who sensed that the master could see what he was thinking. He nodded with a feeling of pride.

Monsieur Léopold cooked them some soup, and when they had finished eating in silence, he leaned back and lit his pipe again. He was contemplating the tiger, and his lively eyes took on a melancholy expression. He looked at Latour.

'I came to Paris with my brother when I was twenty-two.'

Latour was startled. It was the first time a grown man had ever confided anything to him. Why was he talking to him like this, what could he want? But there was something in Léopold's eyes and tone of voice that suggested he might be talking to himself, Latour's presence being just an excuse.

'Our father was still quite well off then and had obtained a place for me at university. I lived in the Rue St Jacques, right by the medical faculty building and the anatomy theatre in the Jardin du Roi. I was obsessed with knowing everything about the internal organs and the workings of the body. What's underneath, what's hidden behind this flimsy skin of ours? I read everything I could find. I discovered the Renaissance painters' interest in anatomical dissection. Did you know that Michelangelo spent twelve years in the dissecting chamber studying the human form? He knew where every organ was, knew every sinew in the human hand.'

Léopold gripped Latour's hand and dug his fingers into it as if to emphasize his meaning. Latour looked from the master's hand up into his elated eyes.

'Go on.'

'The Royal Surgeon taught us in the anatomy theatre, with demonstrations and dissections. I worked day and night to be the best pupil of that strict and exacting teacher. Then came the moment when I had to dissect my first cadaver, an old man who had died of a tumour on the brain. I set about dissecting the brain by a particularly challenging method, following the pathways of the nerves to see where they went and where they ended. But the brain itself was so soft and the nerve fibres so fine that I couldn't manage to cut through it without severing them. The demonstration was a failure. Later I worked as a doctor in Paris among people who had enough money to imagine themselves not poor. I performed surgical procedures, I did bleeding. In the evenings I went back to the anatomy theatre in the Jardin du Roi. I wanted that too, I wanted to be a great anatomist, to make a great discovery. But in those days it was very difficult to get hold of suitable corpses. It affected my judgement, you know, I did things I ought not to have done.'

'What did you do, Monsieur?'

'Something that made my work too easy.'

'Monsieur?'

He was silent for a moment.

'I believed anatomy to be more important than anything else. I can still see in my mind's eye the light in the anatomy theatre at night, the reflection of the lamps in the narrow windows. I was mostly alone in there. I would sit half asleep on one of the benches, trying to think of a way to deal with the lack of corpses. As if in a dream I found myself in a cemetery, the Cimetière des Innocents. I started bringing home corpses after dark, my boy. I dissected fresh corpses for months, and it's a miracle I wasn't ill. I gave lectures and was regarded as a promising talent. And then one evening I was cutting into the convolutions of a woman's brain, when I suddenly looked down at the scalpel, at the grey and white substance before me, and cast my eyes over her body: there on her skin were the marks of the infection that had killed her! I dropped my scalpel and fled. It was still late evening, and as I walked across the street to my room, and throughout the rest of that sleepless night, I felt that I had lost myself, my childhood faith, everything my father had taught me. God's merciful will. Now I am not so interested in the human body.'

It had turned to dusk outside, and Latour was afraid Bou-Bou might be getting anxious about him. Léopold too was staring out into the darkness, with a faint smile on his face. Latour felt both touched and ashamed, as if he had gained an insight he had not wanted. He rose slowly from his stool at the workbench. Léopold stretched again, as though shaking himself free of his sobering story.

Still smiling, he said, 'No need to hang about any longer, boy. Get on home with you.'

Latour nodded. But he did not move immediately.

'May I come back another time?'

'I'll be waiting for you tomorrow, my boy, straight after school.'

Latour left the hut in pitch darkness. He stumbled across the yard, and fought his way through the foliage of the trees surrounding the hut. There was a fresh smell of the woods and the sea in the air. He began to run and ran the whole way home. Drawing near, he stopped to look at the stone building and the dull yellow light in Bou-Bou's window. He thought of the tiger's faceless face again, and that he, the ugliest child in the whole of France, was no uglier than anyone else beneath the thin veil of skin.

When he opened the door he expected to be met by Bou-Bou's worried features. But everything was dark. He went up the stairs, and the higher he got the more he could hear of what was going on, Goupils' panting, Bou-Bou's sweet nothings.

'My little chicken.'

'My little song thrush.'

Their behaviour enraged him. How could they? On a day like this, when Monsieur Léopold was stuffing the first tiger in Normandy. He paused half-way up the stairs. The thought of stuffing a human being — how it would feel to stand over a stuffed person, like Goupils, for instance — made the sounds of the couple fade away, and as he crawled under the bed-clothes he could hear nothing but the soft swish of the sea.

Latour and Léopold worked on the tiger for a good two weeks. They cleaned the pelt and tanned it with a mixture of arsenic and alum. They made a clay mould of the body and commenced the painstaking and time-consuming process of creating a model that the pelt could be drawn over. They filled the tiger's folds of skin with tansy and the tobacco from Father

Martin's mysterious parcel and then pulled the pelt over the clay, stretching it with pincers and clamps of various sizes, steaming and dampening it, until finally they reached the stage where Léopold could solemnly sew it up. Latour watched wide-eyed as the pelt closed round its new clay body. With the tiger finally completed, he was struck with a sense of unreality. This had been the object of their labours; but when the tiger was placed before him, Latour thought he must be imagining it.

They positioned the animal in the middle of the floor so that it would be the first thing the captain saw when he came in. They stood admiring it, unsteady on their legs. The ears, lips, eyes, the finely formed skull, the paws, with claws un-sheathed. Real, yet unreal. Natural, yet artificial. There was silence in Léopold's hut. It was as if the tiger's immobility had infected them as they gazed upon the magnificent wild beast with tears in their eyes. But gradually they began to recover. The smell of the corpse, the chaos of bones, all was gone. The pelt was clean, the body perfectly shaped. One paw was held aloft as if to catch a fly. Its neck was flexed. The animal had become alive again. Latour thought it was the most beautiful thing he had ever seen.

*

Latour had been so involved in the work on the tiger that when he was at home again with nothing to do he was sur-prised to find that his mother was simply not there. He had only half-registered, as in a dream, that she was out travelling alone, and that she was away for several days at a time. He had seen the bright glow in her eyes when she came back, the powder on her cheeks, but had not thought anything of it. He had not even asked what she had been doing, where she had been, what was going on. When two days later he found her sitting in the kitchen dunking her bread in her coffee with a totally expressionless face, he stationed himself in the doorway and asked her in a grown-up voice where she had been. He saw the traces of make-up on her face, the stray hairs from a white wig that had got caught in her own grey-brown tangle of hair and for the first time felt concern for her. There was something false, improbable, even repellent in the idea that Bou-Bou was dressing herself up like a fine Madame, that she was putting on expensive dresses and a wig, transforming herself into a lady like any other. He wanted to go over to her and scream at her and call her a sham. But all he said was, 'Where have you been?'

'Nowhere.'

'You must have been somewhere.'

'In Paris.'

'What were you doing there?'

'Nothing.'

'You must have done something.'

'Nothing, I said. Leave me alone.'

'What did you do there?'

'Business. Business, business and more business,'

She pushed past him in the doorway and he noticed a disgusting smell of perfume.

*

Father Martin was an intense man. He lectured on the historical development of the study of anatomy with fiery eyes, and Latour sat listening to him with breathless attention. For the dissection of dogs and apes by the Greeks and Romans, Father Martin had nothing but contempt, and he found Hippocrates' interpretations woeful: he had even confused sinews with nerves and arteries with veins! Father Martin talked of the medical school in Alexandria, founded by Ptolemy the First, where Galen, at least, had come from Rome and produced some decent work. But there was no real development until the fourteenth century. Mondius de Liucci's *Anathomia* was based entirely on the study of human corpses. How could you expect to learn about the internal workings of the human body by cutting up dogs? Was that not turning dogs into humans and humans into dogs? Even donkeys had complicated brains, but that did not make them great thinkers. The pupils laughed. Father Martin raised his voice, and they went quiet.

'That was not God's intention.'

He stopped at that point and paused to gather his thoughts, looking fleetingly round the room. He well knew that the Catholic Church had banned the dissection of human cadavers for several centuries and that it was still a sensitive issue. But he was a rational priest and believed in the unity of education and faith. He straightened his shoulders and then leaned forward to address the class.

'Why are there anatomists? Latour?'

Latour nodded acknowledgement and stood up to answer the question. He raised his head to meet Father Martin's burning gaze and suddenly felt uncertain, even though he had thought the answer was self-evident. Father Martin's expression was like a mirror to his inadequacy, but he summoned up his courage and replied, 'Perhaps so that we can find out what there is under the skin?'

It was during the course of this series of lectures that a terrible thing happened. It was an event that had something pointless and at the same time painfully comical about it.

One spring morning a sick fly settled on Bou-Bou's lip. She was bending over the fish stall in Honfleur inspecting the choice before her — squid, cod, burbot — wondering whether she should ask the stallholder about herring, knowing it was out of season and illegal but knowing too that many an unscrupulous fisherman sold superb herring before daybreak and that the stallholder was very likely to have a few kilos tucked away. She had the taste of young herring on her tongue already at the mere thought of it and she opened her mouth a little as if to draw it in and savour it. And there, resting befuddled on the skin of her lip, sat a sick fly, almost looking as if it were about to fall into her half-open mouth. But then pride, the thought of the fishwife's negative grunt, drove out the dream of herring, and Bou-Bou flicked the fly from her mouth and asked for five small codling instead. The kiss of a fly. It was enough. Purple fever. Faintness, sickness and then purple spots on her neck. Her overweight body swelled up even more, her cheeks turned blue, and one eye closed up. Latour sped into Honfleur. Kicked open the door of Goupils' office and screamed at him to call a doctor, the best doctor in the whole of Normandy, to hurry, there was no time to lose. Goupils stared from Latour to his client, who was sitting gaping in astonishment, and back again. Why? For whom? Latour didn't understand. What for? Who for? 'It's Bou-Bou,' he stammered. What was the matter with her? 'She's come out in spots.' Spots? 'Purple spots, all over her.'

'*Merde*,' Goupils muttered, excusing himself to his client and rushing off with Latour, son and lover side by side. Whether it was fright or sympathy, thoughts of financial disaster, loneliness or motherlessness that made them run, or the imperative of death itself that gave momentum to their headlong race up and down the streets of Honfleur, shouting out the names and addresses of doctors in frenzied disarray, they eventually found a Dr Mezan to drag away from the boy with smallpox he was tending and bundle off in Goupils' carriage.

Dr Mezan took one look at the sick woman, picked up his bag and went out into the hall. Son and lover followed him. Was there nothing he could do? The doctor shook his head. 'Purple fever,' he said. Emphatically. In a doom-laden voice. A shake of the head in unison from Goupils and Latour. Why would he not do something? It was purple fever, the doctor repeated. There was nothing he could do. He was sorry. She had reached the final stage of the illness, had gone into a *coma vigil*, and medical science was at a loss, the doctor said ominously. She would be gone within a few hours. Would they like the priest to be sent for?

They assented, without comprehending, and went back in to Bou-Bou. She was lying gazing at the ceiling with one eye. She did not stir. Her breathing was irregular. Her lips were moving, or rather they were twitching in a way that made them believe she was about to say something that would explain everything for them. They both bent over her, more in perplexity than despair. The woman on the bed no longer even resembled Bou-Bou: her body was bloated and turning blue. Streams of pus poured from her closed eye.

Latour looked at his mother. It was evident that she was in pain, and he realized that if he could not understand what she felt he would afterwards never understand that she no longer existed.

He took her hand. It was hard and swollen. The nails were the only part that still looked like hers. He put his own hands over her cold fingers, thinking she was actually quite beautiful behind all the swelling and blue coloration, and that he would have liked to lie down beside her and cuddle up to her. Goupils cleared his throat. And so did she, the dying woman, in a grotesque parody. She opened her mouth, her lips trembled, and she said, in strong unwavering tones, the second before she died, 'My son!'

It could have sounded like a declaration of love, but Latour thought it was an attempt to humiliate him. Why else should she die in that way? As Goupils drew the sheet up over her and bowed his head in prayer, Latour stood absolutely rigid, staring at the bed. Why had she done this to him?

Someone in the room was speaking.

'I know how terrible it must feel.'

'I'm so sorry.'

'I know how you must be feeling, my boy.'

He stood completely still, and all he could think was that he felt nothing.

Then suddenly he saw the connection. What must have happened. The trips to Paris. The illness. It was obvious: she had been poisoned. That was it. He shut his eyes. Could he just stand there, or would someone soon start talking to him again and upsetting him? He wouldn't be able to take it. He stared down at his mother and suddenly felt giddy. He fell across the bed and the sheet covering his mother's body, choking and vomiting. He pressed his face down into the sheet and smelt the sweet smell of her body. He realized that he was crying, but his only thought was that he had no feelings at all.

2

Leaving Honfleur

M*y* arms are folded across my chest. My eyes are shut tight. The darkness is good. My shoulder-blades against the cold floor. I'm trying not to think of anything; I'm eating nothing, drinking nothing. I'm lying completely still, as if asleep. The darkness is good. I'm famished but I can't eat. I've woken up with cramp. As if someone were cutting into me but with no pain. Just a feeling of disintegration. I keep my eyes shut. Lie completely still. I feel numb. The darkness is good. She's lying on the bed, near me, above me, and I'm thinking how alike we are. I let my imagination take over. She is ill.

'What's the matter?' I ask.

She doesn't reply but lays her big hands on my face. We do things to one another. I press my face into her belly. Touch her. We kiss. Her lips move. I gently stroke her groin, which is hairy, but soft and smooth underneath. I press myself against her. She is ill.

I hear footsteps. They stop. I keep my eyes shut.

The priest says, 'Is the boy all right?'

The sexton replies in a shrill voice, 'He looks very bad.'

'Is he dead?'

'It would certainly appear so. I think he may be gone.'

They advance upon me cautiously. I recognize the sexton's

smell. The priest's cold hand on my neck. And then the sexton's slightly disappointed tone:

'He's alive.'

I got into bed with her that night.

I didn't want them to take her away. I didn't cry. But the priest comforted me. I forced myself to tell them to take her away. They came to fetch her during the afternoon. It was hard work getting her heavy body out of the house, up on to the cart. There was so much of her. The sexton groaned and grumbled and demanded a high fee for the job. I stood watching the cart as it lurched round the sharp bends on its way down to Honfleur and couldn't help thinking they were going to drop her.

I lay on her bed. Visions passing through my mind. Everything at a standstill. All the ships in harbour. Not a cloud in the sky. Colours faded. People without their hair. Stones upturned on the hillside. The earth seared. Houses collapsed, everything shrunken. Nothing left. Just a great expanse of golden sand. A desert. I felt the wind in my face, grains of sand. Not an animal, not a tree, not a human being in sight. The sky merged into the desert. There was nothing out there. But here was I, right in the middle of the desert, with but one thought: poison. Bou-Bou had been poisoned. She had been to Paris and she had been poisoned.

The image of a desert made me vengeful and even hungrier.

I was dirty and quite emaciated by the time I went down into Honfleur to buy some fish. People failed to recognize me. Which didn't bother me. Honfleur stank of half-rotten octopus and lye from the tanneries, a sickly sweet smell everywhere, clinging to everything. I waited in the queue in front of the stall, hungrily eyeing the glistening fish, but could not help wondering where such a nauseating stench could be coming from. The queue snaked between the stalls, between octopus tentacles and pink bellies of cod. Turning round, I found my-self face to face with a prostitute. She had high cheekbones and a protruding upper jaw. She was really ugly. She looked me up and down, condescendingly, brushed a little powder off her nose as if to indicate that my own smell was far from fragrant, then wheezed at me, 'Well?'

I didn't flinch but stood my ground. There was something in her countenance, something I felt the need to decipher. What was it? I had seen her before, outside the tavern in the Rue Haute, surrounded by young men. I had watched her parading brazenly along the quayside. I had gazed in wonder at her high boots. She wore better quality clothes than the other women in Honfleur: hats and wigs and lace and a silver buckle on her posterior. Her name was Valérie.

I was so close to her now that I could detect the odour of sin and debauchery that Father Martin had spoken so much about. She squinted down her nose at me, her thick lips pursed like a snout in a grimace of disgust. Seeing myself reflected in her hatpin, I looked like a beggar. I burst out laughing, unable to control myself, the laughter seeming to tickle my whole body, and I collapsed on the ground laughing as I had never laughed before.

Sales at the fish stall came to a halt. The whore scuttled off.

My master was angry when I went back. He reprimanded me, wanting to know why I hadn't returned before, where I'd been, why I hadn't been there to assist him. I wanted him to strike me, but he didn't.

I had never told Léopold about Bou-Bou, so there was no point in telling him she was dead. I kept quiet. I helped him stuff a few small birds. Minute, precise movements.

'This is very pleasant,' Léopold murmured as he sewed.

Then, speaking louder, 'Look at this beautiful bird, look at it, my boy. Isn't it unbelievable that we've preserved its beauty for a hundred years into the future?'

The body of the little bird made me think of Bou-Bou lying in her coffin, and the idea came to me that perhaps she too ought to be stuffed, because she would grow ugly in her coffin, her body would disintegrate and rot and turn to dust. I knew it would. As I rose to leave, my master gave me another scolding and told me to come back the following day.

But the next day I was ill. I lay on the flagstones outside the cottage vomiting. It didn't hurt, and I liked having the wind in my face, because I was sweating and had no strength in me, no strength at all.

I closed my eyes.

I was flying over the woods. There was my master's hut visible through the canopy of leaves. I landed in the yard. I saw his smiling face at the window. He clapped his hands and opened the door to me, beckoning me in.

'You see that gull on the bottom shelf?'

His eyes were not green today but as blue as my own.

'I want you to have it. As a reward.'

I went over to the bird. Picked it up. Smiled at my master, his face looming above me. I felt quite strong, even though I had flown the whole way there. He took me by the arm and led me through the hut to the bedroom.

'I'm in a generous mood today,' he said, opening the door.

I could make out the shapes of books all over the dimly-lit room. They covered the walls from floor to ceiling, spread across the floor, up on to the windowsill — even the one and only chair in the room was piled high with books.

'So, let me see,' he said, peering round the room, his eyes radiant as if from some inner exaltation. He crossed over to the bookshelves and reached up to select a thick tome.

'I got this book in Paris, from the King's personal physician.'

He weighed it in his hand, turning and caressing it. He tousled my hair and suddenly I found the heavy volume in my possession. I turned it as he had done and read the cover. Andreas Vesalius. *De Humani Corporis Fabrica.*

'It's for you, my boy.'

His face shone in the semi-darkness.

'And this one, my son.'

Raymond de Vieussens' *Neurographia Universalis.* I put the two volumes under my arm. We stood for a while longer among the books in that strange stillness. Then we went back to the workshop, and I emerged from his hut with the books under one arm and the gull under the other.

I left Léopold in his narrow bed, where he had fallen into a deep sleep.

On my way home I stopped in the middle of the woods among the dense trees and looked into the gull's eyes. It seemed not to be dead, just immobile, trapped for all eternity in its bird's body.

I felt that I would never again be able to return to my master's hut.

The whole of that spring I lay in bed contemplating the gull that I had christened Caesar. I would laugh to myself and then lapse into silence. That was how it was all spring. Memories of events, things people had said, all revolving round in my brain. But nothing stuck. And nothing seemed important. I was not unhappy. But nor was I happy. Strange as it may seem, it was as if I were not alive.

I stared at Caesar. The expression in his eyes had altered now. It looked as if he were scanning the seas for herring. I gazed into his little eyes for a long time and thought I could see the rapaciousness in them. Had Caesar been killed as he was about to catch a herring in his beak? It was an uncomfortable thought. I often went to sleep with Caesar on my chest. One night I dreamt that I woke up and couldn't move. In my dream I had the notion that I would not be able to move until I said a particular word, but I didn't know what it was. That single word would save me, but I was unable to find it.

Vesalius' book was full of fantastic diagrams. You could see right inside the bodies, all the muscles and blood vessels in a human body. An extraordinarily complicated weave. I sat spellbound, gasping at the exquisite draughtsmanship. People without skin. Beneath their fine skin people were complex patterns, fabulous machines. The drawings were almost terrifyingly detailed. Would I ever be able to look at a human being again without thinking of these diagrams, without thinking of the patterns under the skin?

That was all that was left of Bou-Bou now.

Bone, muscles, blood vessels, nerves, internal organs. Vesalius wrote about all those things. He rejected the anatomy of previous eras. But for me the diagrams were the most entrancing aspect of the whole book.

The brain was an enigma to him. He could explain the body, but when he wrote about the brain, he simply posed questions. He discounted older theories about the existence of chambers. He rejected the concept of their being the seat of the soul, and that the senses, reason and memory emanated from these fluid-filled spaces. But he went no further than that. Did he know nothing of the brain? The book contained the first-ever drawing of the brain's soft matter, the convolutions and nerves entangled around each other. How strange to think that something so contorted could have been regarded as the seat of the soul.

Was pain one of the senses? Where was the seat of pain?

I lay reading that wonderful book by the great Vesalius all through the spring, his drawings vivid in my mind's eye well into the night.

When I went out I was rather apprehensive about meeting people who might want to start talking about Bou-Bou. What would I say? If they expressed their sorrow, I would know they didn't mean it and what would I say then? Or what if they demanded money? Bou-Bou owed not a sou to anyone, but I was sure there were many who would assert that she did. Should I say she wasn't dead? Should I tell them she couldn't be dead because I hadn't felt anything when she died? Would they understand that?

Goupils came to our cottage. He avoided my eyes when he introduced the subject of the business, so I stopped listening to what he had to say. I heard his voice as if it were just a noise, the rumble of a cart or the sound of the sea in the morning. But I understood some of it. The situation was roughly this: there was no will, and so in accordance with the contract he had drawn up with Bou-Bou all the assets of the company passed to Goupils. He showed me a sheet of paper with a signature on, but I didn't read it, just stared at it. The letters didn't look like letters. They flowed into one another, mere dots on the surface, like the stippling made by rain in the sand.

'But I feel a responsibility for you, Latour, and I don't want to seem unreasonable.'

So he promised not to lay claim to any valuables in the cottage itself. I could hardly suppress a wan smile. After the murder attempt Bou-Bou had made it a rule never to keep anything of value on the premises, and Goupils knew as well as I did that the only valuable item there was the old casket she had inherited from her parents.

I watched him as he went off down the winding path. At the edge of the wood he turned to look back up at the cottage.

I don't think he saw me, because he lingered for some time. I recalled the occasion when he had tied me to the tree in the garden without punishing me, and the power I'd once felt he had over me. Now I was observing him and it seemed to me that he no longer existed.

One day I saw a young woman, a housemaid, being whipped outside St Catherine's Church for stealing food. She was whipped so brutally that the flesh fell off her in strips. Her screams were terrible to hear. I had to turn away, feeling sick yet also aroused.

Was that how I wanted to scream?

When summer came, I started catching butterflies again. I found some really good ones and put them in the killing jar. I came upon Léopold in the woods and tried to hide from him, but he saw me. I wanted to run away, but when he called my name, I couldn't. I stayed where I was, and he came over to me, put his hand on the nape of my neck, and I felt his calloused skin on mine. He wasn't angry. Why not? I don't know. He ruffled my hair and asked me about the butterflies. We went back to his hut. I couldn't take my eyes from Caesar's empty place on the shelves and the closed door to the bedroom. I stole a glance at Léopold: had he not noticed that the gull had gone? I thought everything would be changed, but Léopold was still the same.

He helped me catalogue the butterflies and pin them on to boards. I found a red admiral one morning asleep on the trunk of a tree — by pure luck: it had folded its wings together and the undersides were exactly the same colour as the bark. For several minutes I held my breath, spellbound by the similarity of butterfly and bark. It was remarkable. Having caught it I decided not to kill it. I got a birdcage from Léopold, released the admiral into it and watched it flap around on its beautiful wings. I stared at it in wonder, as it gradually accustomed itself to being a prisoner. It settled on the rotting apples at the bottom of the cage. I imagined that its tiny specks of eyes were pleading with me and that it acknowledged me as its lord and master.

One evening when Léopold was sitting drinking calvados sweetened with sugar he told me about the whores of Honfleur and about Valérie, the ugly one, the one I knew, the one I had behaved so unaccountably towards. He really enthused about her, praising her anatomy, her hipbones and elbows, her navel and her cheekbones, the curve of her spine, her knuckles, her high insteps and her nipples. He talked about the length of her muscles, her calves, her ligaments, gesticulating all the time as he did so.

'By Jove, my boy, what thighs. What a rump. What breasts, what a belly! She's got the perfect anatomy.'

He stopped, pursing his lips. I wanted him to continue so I poured him some more of the spirit.

'But you soon tire of a beautiful landscape,' he said wistfully, setting his glass on the table. 'After a while you behold the trees and meadows with sadness and remember how stimulating the view once was. And when you meet a stranger who is obviously passionate about the same landscape you look at him in disbelief and shrug your shoulders and mumble half-hearted agreement before wearily wending your way home. Only when a bolt of lightning crashes into a tree and leaves a blemish on the landscape is your previous enthusiasm rekindled, and you bristle with indignation. How dare something so ugly intrude, you think. But the truth is that you have a secret craving for ugliness and devastation, because they teach you to appreciate the scene you have grown bored with. That's how it is with Valérie. You can admire the curve of her belly and the golden tint of her pubic hair, you can cast your eyes over her firm thighs and make yourself breathless with excitement contemplating her calves and feet. But after a while you tire. So what, you think. You yawn and stretch and just want to get it done with. Then she leans over you, and you catch the smell of her breasts, and she shoves her ugly face right in front of yours, whispering something foul, something outrageous, and you're filled with passion again. So into bed you go. And as you're thrusting into her, furious with desire, you realize she's tricked you again, and that you're a slave to her ambivalent charms.'

I had let my imagination take over as he spoke. I could see her before me and, closing my eyes, I dreamt that I had hoisted her up by a hook in the ceiling and was drawing on her body with a quill pen. She was whimpering, and the quill was tearing the fine skin on her belly as she hung there helpless. When I opened my eyes, I discovered that Léopold had stopped talking and was sitting scrutinizing me.

That night the image of the hanging woman came back to me in my dreams. I woke up feeling giddy. Sick and happy. It was an emotion I had no name for, that terrified me as much as aroused me.

And then I was standing pressing my cheek against the bark of a tree, staring towards the tavern in the Rue Haute. There she came, the whore, Valérie. She really did have the ugliest face in the whole of Honfleur. But she certainly also had the perfect anatomy, a tall delectable figure. I had a powerful urge to run across the road, to catch her and admire her body, to hold her captive. But I couldn't move. It was as if I had no strength, as if I were a baby again, unable to walk. I went on watching her, trying to forget how small I felt.

I had seen the whores strutting up and down the Rue du Daphne. I had seen the young lads kissing them in the street and serenading them, while at dusk married men skulked past close up against the houses, their faces hidden behind upturned collars. But only recently had I realized what they were actually doing. I had read in Bou-Bou's books about fallen women but found it unbelievable that there were any here, in the middle of Honfleur.

I thought I could discern Valérie's smell, the aroma of burnt sugar. I wondered if I should get up and go: the tugging sensation in my chest was not a good sign, and Father Martin would be angry if he could see me. But I remained where I was, staring so intently that I made my eyes water. She was standing nonchalantly in a doorway looking up and down the street, wiggling her bottom a little. When a carriage came by she climbed into it and drove off. I felt absolutely tiny and slunk behind a tree. To wait.

*

My knuckles made a hollow sound as I rapped. There was only an inch or so of rotten wood between her and me. I heard shoes crossing the floor. A misshapen, sleepy face peered round the door. I straightened up — I was wearing one of Goupils' old jackets with a high split back, his knee-breeches and slightly too large shoes with silver buckles — swallowed hard and showed her the leather purse of gold coins from Bou-Bou's casket. I looked expectantly at her gaunt and weary features, at her grey eyes. The clock had just struck twelve, but her expression suggested it was the middle of the night. She slowly opened the door and let me slip inside. The room was scantily furnished; it smelt of soap and male sweat.

We faced each other across the void. On the far wall hung a few portraits and sketches of animals. Did she sketch? Three tom-cats were asleep on a pouffe in one corner of the room.

Valérie stood there in her loose housecoat observing me, the cords swirling about her body like restless clouds. Part of a breast, the curve of her thigh, her long muscles. She seemed sad, and her smile did little to counteract the impression.

Did the smile belong to someone else?

She stroked the inside of my arm, her nails scratching me, tickling. She pushed me down into a chair by the side of the bed, and I sat there transfixed by her small hands as they untied the braids of her housecoat, imagining I could already smell the caramel fragrance of her vagina. I let my eyes follow the contours of her body, her belly and her dark earthy-brown nipples, her neck. I thought of Léopold's fulsome words and felt my precocious penis creeping along my thigh like a damp worm. My exploratory gaze ended at her face: she had round cheeks the strange colour of putrefied fish, a mixture of pink and blue. Her voice was surprisingly deep.

'What's your name?'

I looked at her without replying.

'I'm Valérie Sevran,' she said in a tone that suggested an intimate confidence.

She continued to loosen the braids of her housecoat.

'Monsieur Léopold sent me,' I murmured. I could tell I was muttering and blushing and not making myself properly understood. 'He's too old to come himself but he wants some measurements of a beautiful woman for his anatomical studies. All you have to do is lie still, as if you were dead. You'll get two gold coins for it.'

She snorted, whether in derision or encouragement I wasn't sure, and turned her back on me, peeling her housecoat inordinately slowly off her shoulders. Perhaps that was part of her technique, prolonging, confusing, making men frustrated with impatience; or perhaps it was the only power she had over them.

Her bottom came into view, a dark crack between two delightful hemispheres, and she turned and lay on the bed. I looked at her toes, her crooked little toe, the down of delicate golden hair that covered her legs, let my gaze wander up to her knees, admired her finely honed kneecaps and thigh muscles. She shut her eyes, a mocking smile on her lips. How beautiful she was. She drew her long nails over my knee, pulled me closer, my member throbbed. She smelt of sleep. I took out the tape-measure and bent over her to read the exact measurements of the triangle between her nipples and her mouth, staring hard at the tape. As it touched her brown nipple at one end and her lips at the other, I noticed how still she kept, as if she were far away, in a deep slumber. I measured her thighs, her knees. Her belly and hips. The distance between her mouth and her groin. When I had taken all the measurements, I wrote them down in a notebook. My task was complete. I sat back in the chair and heard how heavily I was breathing. She opened her eyes and gave me a sardonic grin. She could hardly have much confidence in my story, I thought, and probably didn't believe it, but her grin sent a delightful shiver through my whole body. I returned her smile, and to me her mouth looked like a butterfly with outspread wings.

And then she leaned forward over me and put her hand with its long fingernails down inside my breeches and scratched me and squeezed me and dug her nails into me, and I knew it ought to hurt, but I felt it only as a gentle tickle. And then my senses began to reel.

On my way home the women in the marketplace glowered at me as usual. I knew what they were thinking: 'That bloody moneylender's son.'

'Fossil face!'

The harsh voice of a boatbuilder yelled after me, but I pretended not to hear. I observed the activities of the market women and the boatbuilders as if from a great height. As I walked up the path to Bou-Bou's cottage I had a sudden vision of myself in a coach bound for Paris. And I thought to myself: 'You can't stay here. Honfleur can go to Hell.'

Entering the cottage, Bou-Bou's cottage, I went to the trunk that contained her clothes. I lifted the lid, and the sweet scent of her body rose towards me. I took out her clothes and laid them on the floor. Right at my feet was the embroidered dress with ruched ribbon that she had worn on that final trip to Paris. I picked it up, and there, tucked between the folds of the smooth back, I found a piece of paper. Dropping the dress to the floor, I opened it.

There were eight names on it, eight names of men and women, and with every name I read I became increasingly convinced that every single one of them was responsible for Bou-Bou's death. These were the names, in Bou-Bou's uneven handwriting, one after another, with gaps between, as if to emphasize the significance of their presence on the list:

La Boulaye, opera singer

Monsieur Jacques, textile manufacturer

Denis-Philippe Moette, natural historian and encyclopædist

Comte de Rochette

Father Noircuill, Benedictine monk

Madame Arnault, seamstress

Jean Foubert, tannery owner

Président de Curval.

*

I met her again, by the market stalls. She pulled a face and turned her back on me. I felt exhilarated and followed her down the street. In the alley leading to her room, in the dark shadow behind the bell-tower above the old inn, she suddenly stopped and waited for me to catch her up. Then she flew into a temper at my following her, asked me why I didn't go home to my mother, why I didn't feel ashamed of myself. I stood on tiptoe and whispered, 'You're right, Mademoiselle, I am a rogue, a shameless lout. But I'm an admirer of yours and I have one or two interesting proposals to make.'

My tongue felt numb in my mouth, and I don't think she understood what I said. I smiled at her, tried to say more but couldn't, my mouth wouldn't obey. I pulled my leather purse out of my pocket and showed it to her, but she just stared at me in silence. Then she began to laugh.

I had spent the nights letting my imagination run riot. I had invented my own language.

'I want to draw on your body,' I said.

Her face seemed even more crooked, as she raised a quizzical eyebrow.

But she would let me do it. As long as I paid.

She lay on her bed, and I drew on her with the sharp quill pen, marking the outlines of her breasts and hipbones, pretending to myself that I was cutting into her and imagining I could hear her screams. I looked into her grey eyes, and they seemed empty, an empty expression that excited me. My whole body went cold. The worm crept along my thigh, leaving a streak of slime. It was a wonderful way to experience cold, almost like pain.

Then she removed my breeches and scratched me till I bled and ejaculated all over her face.

Afterwards we sat one on either side of the big table in the kitchen and drank *café au lait*.

'A habit I picked up in Paris.'

Valérie herself also liked drawing. Quick violent lines that initially resembled nothing more than a scribble. But then suddenly a face would emerge on the paper. I think my ugly mug pleased her, because she sketched it from every conceivable angle.

I drew on her. And she drew me. While she drew, I told stories. Stories I had heard from Léopold, about animals he had stuffed, about journeys to Africa and the Orient. She was impressed with the way I told them. But they were only my master's words, and sometimes I didn't understand what I was saying myself; I was just very good at imitating him. Valérie listened, with a sad smile. It was as if I could mould her with words. When I left she said *au revoir*. And I came back. Everything she did and said, her glances, her sketches of my face, everything made me feel we would soon be leaving Honfleur together, and I would be able to start a whole new life.

She spoke to me of times gone by. About Paris. About brothels and aristocrats and all she had seen and learnt. About Les Halles and the Palais-Royal and the Hôtel-Dieu. Her face became more animated whenever she talked about Paris, a flush creeping over her cheeks, her head raised high. She enjoyed going for walks and wanted me to go with her to the hills above the town.

'Look at the sea!'

I went along, even though I didn't care for the view. Because I liked to hear her talk about Paris.

People gave us peculiar glances. The women shouted after Valérie in their coarse voices: 'Witch! Evil-Eye!' She stayed indoors increasingly, going to the fish stalls really early in the morning before it was light. She asked me to buy bread and vegetables for her. She began to fear the women. She said she had bad dreams and an ominous feeling that something disastrous was about to occur.

I had soon exhausted all the money in Bou-Bou's casket. I had drawn so much on Valérie's body that she could no longer get any other clients. I had scratched circles round her nipples so deep that she screamed, and it thrilled me to hear those screams. She did the same to me, with her nails, and then she would kiss me on the face and tell me she liked me, but of course I didn't believe her. I lay gazing up at the clouds and the hilltops, my cheek against her warm belly. I came so close to feeling pain.

I am standing alone in the middle of Bou-Bou's cottage. It is night, and my eyes are shut as I try to remember the furniture that once stood here, Bou-Bou's clothes, her account books. It is all fading from my mind; I can't remember things, can no longer recognize things. I stand here enveloped in my own darkness, with one clear and dominant thought in my head.

I must go to Paris. That's where I shall find out the nature of pain.

*

But it was Goupils, eternally devious, who was to send me away from Honfleur.

Goupils did not like the rumours about Valérie and me and decided to put a stop to it: we were not good for business. He was her landlord, and one afternoon he came marching straight into her room and said that business was bad and he regretted he had to give her notice to quit. Her accommodation was to be converted into a storeroom for provisions.

'You can stay for a few more days before you return to Paris,' he said as he closed the door politely behind him.

I lay in Bou-Bou's cottage, dreaming once again about Goupils. He was a king. He had a carriage drawn by twelve horses. Every morning he traversed his realm to survey his possessions. And every morning he crouched on his haunches and smelt the grass and rubbed the soil of his own land between his fingers. The very skies above his lands were his. He wanted to walk naked across all he owned. I was a boy with ideas above my station. I sat in a tree with knives in my belt. I slept in the tree and dreamt about how I would employ them. How I would do away with him. By as slow a method as possible, I thought. Then one morning his lackeys found the king in the fields, hacked into little pieces. I woke up in my tree, and my knives were clean. I had never felt so empty.

A few days later, with the sun bright in the sky, I walked down to Valérie, my mind seething with ideas. Should we rob Goupils? And go to Paris? How about it? Valérie knew where he kept his valuables. She thought it would be no problem for me, being so skinny, to squeeze in through one of his windows. To which I replied that it most certainly would not.

I stood concealed behind some empty wine barrels, staring up at Goupils' house. His lamp was lit, and he was dressed in a carnival costume. There was to be a masquerade ball at Madame de Plessis' that evening. Having eaten to excess and drunk brandy to match, flirted with the young ladies of Honfleur and pinched their breasts, he would probably make his way to the house of a common whore and spend the night there as usual. I thought of Goupils' body, his miserable little penis and how happy he would be with the whore. As it got darker, I dozed off amidst the aroma of rancid wine. When I awoke, everything was in darkness. I crossed the square and crept along the side of the house and into the yard at the rear.

I freed the window catch with a knife and was soon inside. Up the red staircase to Goupils' luxurious bedroom.

'They say he has a casket of jewels nailed down under the bed, the old skinflint. We could get to Paris on the strength of one piece,' Valérie had said.

I entered the room. A figure lay in the bed.

I stood perfectly motionless. Goupils was sleeping, a blue shadow across his face. He had a shabby nightcap on his balding head. Had he returned while I was asleep and dreaming behind the wine barrels? I waited, holding the knife in my hand. I imagined him waking and the knife slashing his face, opening up his features like a door. A shiver of anticipation coursed through my veins. Then Goupils opened his eyes but did not stir. He observed me dully as if unaware that he was awake. Everything was absolutely quiet. I wanted to move, to speak, to act. But something restrained me. It was totally silent. The king in his bed had created the silence. He was lord of the silence, he owned it. I was trapped by his unseeing gaze. I could not breathe. The king's eyes blinked. And then closed again. I stood watching him, waiting for him to sit up, say something, give me the opportunity to use the knife and see his pain. But he lay in the bed unmoving, fast asleep. For him I was nothing but a dream.

Crawling under the bed, I found the jewels, exactly as expected. I had another look at the man in the bed, his idiotic nightcap, his somnolent features, and went back down the staircase to his office. As I struck my tinderbox over his papers, I inadvertently set fire to my jacket. For a moment I just stared at the flames creeping up my arm. I could feel the heat from my wrist to my elbow. Would I also feel pain? The fire caught the desk and account books and started raging around me, enveloping me. I could see my skin through the burning sleeve of my jacket, crinkling up, blistering, reddening. But all I could feel was heat. I ripped off the jacket in anger, threw it into the flames and ran out of the office.

Wriggling through the window I found myself on the square again and stood under a tree to watch the flames licking at the windowpanes. I had a taste of iron in my mouth, and it was a few seconds before I realized I had bitten my tongue and made it bleed while I was in the office. I was breathing quickly and heavily. The thought occurred to me that now I could do exactly what I wanted, and I felt an impulse to write in the earth with the toe of my shoe so that someone would know what had happened here. But then I heard a crash above, and from the other side of the house the sound of Goupils' voice.

'Fire! My house is on fire!'

And I whispered to myself. 'It's on fire. Monsieur Goupils' house is on fire.'

I turned and walked calmly away down the street. The air was full of ash and apple blossom.

3

Paris

*T*he roads in those days were in a parlous condition. The coach taking Valérie and Latour from Honfleur to Paris bumped along at an average speed of five kilometres an hour. Their route, an unmarked dirt track meandering through the countryside, was full of potholes, and the wheels kept sinking into the water and mud. Pedestrians and domestic animals with any sense would clamber up the edges as high as they could get. For most travellers the journey was at best an arduous trial of endurance.

Inside the coach, Latour was hemmed in between a preacher and the corpulent wife of a baker. The latter kept up a resonant snoring, while the former intoned continuously from a book of hymns he had written himself. His voice sounded like the grunting of a badger. Opposite him sat Valérie, mumbling in her sleep. Latour was not disturbed by the noises, nor was he frustrated by the slowness of the journey. His wrinkled face had an air of repose about it, his sea-blue eyes stared straight down: he was concentrating.

His gaze was fixed on the book on his lap, Vieussens' *Neurographia Universalis*, which was absorbing the whole of his attention. His mind was no longer on Honfleur or Goupils' burning house. He felt totally unconcerned and not so inordinately small. In his sooty clothing he could easily have been taken for a chimney sweep's boy, but as he read he was experiencing the intoxication of power and freedom.

Vieussens wrote about the brain's white matter and nerve fibres. He described the difference between the white and the grey matter of the cerebrum. The white matter he postulated as consisting of various types of long fibres resembling a sponge-like body through which the spirit flowed in inexplicable ways. That was his theory. So the human body, thought Latour, was rather as if tied together by long strings, and they were all gathered together in the brain into one large knot. He wondered how pain could move from the body to the brain. He had noticed, for instance, that it often took a moment before people felt pain from blows. What happened in the short period of time between Father Martin's cane hitting a boy's backside and the resultant cry? He read on.

In the end his eyes were so tired that the letters began to blur into each other. He looked up from the book. It was evening. The baker's wife was snoring more gently, and the preacher too had fallen asleep. The coach was moving faster.

La Boulaye. Opera singer. Opera singer? What was an opera singer? What was an opera? La Boulaye. The name had a musical resonance in the mouth. La Boulaye. Laaaaa Bouuuuulaaaayyyeee.

Latour sat up straight in the hard seat. By craning forward he could see the coachman's curved back and the hat down over the nape of his neck. Latour was travelling in order to escape from Honfleur, but what he was thinking of, as the carriage jolted along, was not Bou-Bou, Goupils or the fishmarket. He was thinking of unknown bodies. He could see their skin and their heads, their dissected brains.

Beside him on the seat was Caesar, the old gull. He had packed some essentials in the leather bag at his feet: a box of anatomical instruments, anatomy books, Goupils' jewels, a few basic clothes.

And Bou-Bou's list of eight names. That was all he had brought with him. There were a lot of things left in Bou-Bou's house, but he had no use for them. He had all he needed.

He peered out at a succession of textile mills, rows of cider barrels, shacks and mud huts, landowners' mansions. He was leaving Honfleur, and the whole of Normandy, and it felt as if he had been waiting for this moment all his life. But when he closed his eyes to try to sleep, his thoughts were troubled.

La Boulaye. He would find out her address. Rue . . . so and so . . . number . . . such and such . . . Stand in her elegant garden. Listen to her singing. Study this graceful creature. A beautiful woman. A beautiful voice. He would not be in a hurry, he would take his time.

Latour had high expectations of Paris. The Hôtel de Ville, Île de la Cité, and the dreaded Bastille. The names were positively redolent of grandeur and dignity, or so it seemed to him. But when the next morning he opened the carriage door on to his new life he was bemused. The day was only just dawning, a buzz of voices, a cock crowing, the smell of the city, of smoke and people and vegetables. Latour stared about him. Les Halles. The market of markets. He stood absolutely still. Where were the resplendent merchants and the fashionable ladies? The city's renowned *style*, from Valérie's stories. Where were Voltaire, the King's vassals, the farmers proudly displaying their legs of lamb? He looked down at the muddy ground.

'Fresh cod from Honfleur! Cod, fresh cod!'

The fish merchant was bellowing, a dog was regurgitating entrails beneath his stall, wisps of fog drifted through the market.

'Cod from Honfleur! Lovely cod!'

He moved away from the cacophony, taking it all in. There was a dingy brown aura over the tawdry stalls and the produce spread out on the wooden benches. The stallholders' faces looked gaunt and haggard. Where was the *real* market?

'Fresh cod from Honfleur, for Christ's sake!'

Latour found himself looking straight down the man's throat. All about him the vendors were crying their wares to the heavens, even though the customers had not yet arrived. The crass shrieking, the filth, the stench, the mess — it all seemed like a total distortion of the Paris he had expected, a world turned upside down.

He gazed out over the teeming city before him. His face twisted into a childish grimace, a sense of helpless astonishment in his eyes. *What was all this?* Valérie had to drag him away.

They had arrived in Paris in the early spring. They had agreed not to sell Goupils' jewels before they found jobs and accommodation. This arrangement was intended to protect themselves. Valérie had promised that she had plenty of contacts and that it would not be difficult to find work for both of them. But it was not long before they landed up in front of a brothel madam who hardly deigned to raise her eyes from beneath her enormous wig to dismiss them. No one had any use for them.

They slept under bushes and in churchyards for three nights, and ate vegetables bought with their last few coins. The bag containing the jewels lay untouched between them. But after the first night, when both of them awoke with nightmares, Latour could no longer sleep. He lay awake staring at the leather bag as if he were expecting it to have a life of its own. On the third night Valérie proposed that they should divide the jewels between them and bury them separately.

The next day they were in luck. Or were they? They obtained employment in Madame Besson's brothel, which was commonly known as 'The Last Resort' and which Valérie had long tried to avoid. Latour, however, was in high spirits.

'What's wrong with it?'

'There's something wrong with it.'

'Yes, but *what's* wrong with it?'

'There just *is* something wrong with it.'

Madame Besson's brothel was tucked in behind the Place de Grève in a terrace of old houses only a hundred yards from the banks of the Seine. It had a seedy air, and the building was in a state of incipient delapidation, as if it might at any time collapse into itself. She had taken it over from the bankrupt Portuguese parfumier Manuel Corona, and had been perfectly satisfied with the facilities until she became aware that the whole house was impregnated with a strong smell of cheap jasmine oil. Even fifteen years afterwards the building was still permeated by the unmistakable odour of Manuel Corona's failed business.

The furniture was shabby and falling apart, and the walls were peeling, but to Latour that was not important. They had a roof over their heads and food to eat. To him, the fact that Madame Besson invited them into her room, served them tea and smiled at him when she offered them work was a sign of the warmest friendship. The whole time he was with her the memory of this gesture was enough to make him ignore his various humiliations. He was not used to that degree of friendliness. Madame Besson herself was a tall woman with lined features, dressed in a creamy-white loosely flowing dress, her round face chalky white with powder. Rumour had it that she was eighty years old and that it was only thanks to an Austrian quack doctor that she was still alive at all. The miracle was achieved with the aid of the breath of young women, after the Hermippus method. Valérie was allocated a room on the second floor, while Latour was given a bench in the corridor and a blanket to cover him. But it was good enough for him. He was pleased that Madame Besson seemed so kind. And honourable. He thought of her smile, and was content.

There were thirteen whores lodging in Madame Besson's brothel. The youngest was fourteen and the eldest forty-six. In Latour's eyes these jaded women were endlessly fascinating. He could hardly take his eyes off their bedaubed bodies. Powder, wigs, frills, décolletés, corsets, petticoats, shoes — all designed to accentuate their figures. Their breasts spilled out of their bodices, their boots enhanced their calf muscles, their powder emphasized the contours of their necks. He loitered about the corridors, peering in through half-open doors. Thirteen different pairs of nipples. In different sizes. With variations in colour from dark brown to ochre yellow. Thirteen different bellies. Thirteen different pairs of buttocks. Thirteen different groins. Thirteen navels.

He loved watching them. So many movements. He loved watching their bellies and necks in motion. He would stand on the stairs to view the bodies in the salon beneath. Listen to the obscenities, the laughter. See the disdain in their faces. They writhed and twisted, their bodies sore and aching. Thighs. Arms. Necks and jaws. And closer, in the shadows: a vein, a wrinkle. A twitch. So aroused by all this. So small. Such wide eyes.

Madame Besson had a nose for business and had discovered a way of attracting the monied classes. At her establishment there were no limits to the clients' debauchery. Anything could be bought at Madame Besson's. Aristocrats smeared themselves with jam, they paraded around in women's clothes with feathers up their backsides. They drank themselves senseless and dressed up as priests. Urine was served in long-stemmed wine glasses. Servants begged to be suspended from the ceiling. They roared with laughter when the girls farted at them or punished them by performing simple rituals from Madame's own manual entitled *Pain & Delight*. Here the wealthy could walk their nervous, often preposterous tight-rope between shame and lust, far removed from the problems of state finance or family reputation.

Madame Besson's house was special. Was it really the case that the more affluent the clients the more incomprehensible their desires? Latour puzzled over that, but Valérie thought it blindingly obvious. She held the aristocracy in total contempt.

'You only have to think of the rumours about the King and little boys. And of the Comte de Charlois who used a lighted candle on a pregnant woman . . . or of the houses in Arcueill where the rich dine off plates embellished with designs of women and goats . . . or the dreadful Marquis de Sade who whipped poor Jeanne Testard till she bled as he cursed the Almighty . . . , or . . .'

Valérie had a propensity to detachment that enabled her to express moral outrage at something she herself indulged in without it seeming contrived or hypocritical. It was as if another part of her were talking. Latour noted the curl of her lip, her grey eyes. Could she not see she was behaving like a comedy actress? He could not bear to look at her. He sat listening to her harsh voice and felt bored, though gradually his embarrassment faded: some of her remarks sounded serious and heartfelt. He looked up at her, not hearing what she was saying but fixing his eyes on her lips. Without the sound, it was as if they were appealing for help. The image that came to him was of someone sticking pins into her soul.

One morning Latour was sent for by Madame Besson. She bowed and regarded him inquisitively. She smelt of sweet wine. The room was decorated in her own creamy-white colours; her dress blended into the background, making her look infinitely larger.

'The wealthy gentlemen of this city, aristocrats and judges, customs officers and courtiers, men of money and power, they all come here on a journey into a world of fantasy, away from everything they can no longer bear,' she declared with a sniff and a gesture indicating the brothel's comprehensive perfection.

'Everything is permitted in this house. There are no constraints here, no taxes, no unjust penalties. Here they can cast off responsibility, the burden of duties. They will not be called to account by the law, by the people or by the Palace. So — on the one hand, there,' she pointed towards the salon, 'they have all the possibilities in the world. On the other hand, here,' and she put her hand to her breast, 'we have the unspoken rules. Because without rules there can be no freedom, no world of fantasy. Your job, Latour, is to assist Alphonse in the measures he has to employ to keep these doors open.'

She gave Latour a sharp look before leaning forward and kissing his face with her wet mouth.

Her pockmarked nephew, Alphonse, the man with the responsibility for keeping the doors open, was often to be heard trudging along the corridors in his heavy boots.

'Who is this boy?' he growled whenever he saw Latour.

'This is Latour. Madame engaged him herself,' the girls would reply. He would look Latour up and down a few times, somewhat nonplussed, and go on his way muttering to himself. Latour would nod and bow, attempting a smile. But Alphonse would no longer be paying any heed to him. Only when Latour did something wrong, offended against the rules or overstepped some unwritten regulation, did Alphonse accord him any attention. Then his dull eyes would light up, and he would flog Latour with a razor-sharp ox-leather whip. But if Alphonse was a man of limited intellect, he had a fertile imagination as far as the effectiveness of punishment was concerned, and soon realized the boy felt nothing. With an artist's inventiveness he changed tactics and forced Latour to clean his boots with his tongue. The uppers and the soles.

The work consisted of carrying out Alphonse's orders. Helping him with the cleaning, polishing and administration, so that everything ran smoothly. If a client lost control of himself and became unruly in his passion, knocking a girl unconscious or running amok with his member in a flower vase, Latour had the task of diverting any such clowning into new games. He would fetch a club from under the back stairs and give the man a hefty blow on the head. Then he would drag him to the rear courtyard, heave him into a carriage and drive him out to Clamart, the paupers' graveyard. It would take the unfortunate adventurer a long time to regain his ardour after waking up among the bodies enveloped in sacks or in an open grave full of dismembered corpses. Latour had no pangs of conscience. It was a job that paid and actually the most enjoyable one in the brothel.

Latour lay on his bench in the corridor, staring up at the ceiling, wide awake. He was endeavouring to find something on which to focus his thoughts. He studied the cracked walls and the ceiling above him until he could no longer distinguish the individual boards, and then fell asleep. When he awoke, it was still the middle of the night, and he was in some discomfort, feeling faint and unpleasantly sick. His head was completely empty. He knew that if he did not find something to occupy his mind, he would walk out into the street one day and just come to a halt and never move again. He jumped up from his bench.

He went through the items in his bag and found the list of names. In the weak glimmer from the skylight above he read them once more and repeated them until he knew them by heart. Then he tore the piece of paper into shreds, put them in his mouth and swallowed them. Lying down on the bench again he thought that Bou-Bou's final wish would have been for vengeance. Hardly had he formed the thought, however, than it was gone, as if his brain had suddenly ceased to function, and he fell into a deep and refreshing sleep.

In a bookshop in Montmartre he made some interesting finds. He purchased a translation of Mondius de Liucci's *Anathomia*, that Father Martin had once talked about at school in Honfleur. He also bought Richardius' little book on anatomy and some articles by the Danish anatomist Winsløv. Monsieur Léopold had spoken of the Dane with great respect, and so Latour ploughed through them. He liked to think he had learnt something about anatomy, and that he knew a bit about muscles and nerves, the senses and humours and the brain. The long sentences and Latin terms made him agreeably drowsy. He often lay on the bench squinting in the poor light until he finally dropped off to sleep with the book over his face.

Valérie was given a better room, since her ugly face and beautiful body were proving very popular. It had curtains and a carpet on the floor. And she had her own bidet. Latour was allowed into her room from time to time. He loved lying on her bed, dreaming. About the list in his head. About the bodies behind the names. The cavities in the bodies. The mystery of pain.

He became a slave to Alphonse. He had to put up with his mutterings, clean his boots and pick the lice out of his hair. Alphonse was full of contempt. He was contemptuous of the nymphomaniac Queen and the grasping priests, he despised the aristocracy, landowners, police spies and fundamentally he despised Madame Besson and the entire brothel and the girls and even his own job. Latour got tired of listening to him. He imitated him in his own head, repeating phrases to himself, practising the contemptuous tone. When Alphonse was out drinking, Latour would often introduce himself as Master Alphonse to the guests, talking in his grating voice, strutting around in his jacket and intoning his stories with disconcerting verbal mimicry. The girls were highly amused and called him the Parrot.

Whenever the opportunity arose, Latour would explore the city. He strode out, his eyes taking in everything. Staring and staring, even if none of what he saw — boulevards, parks, watchmakers, *parfumeries* — made any special impression on him. He registered buildings and people with a shrug of the shoulders. It was as if he knew that Paris would never mean anything to him. It took a long time before he dared to admit the thought that what he was really searching for was very simple. A debtor. One of the conspirators responsible for Bou-Bou's death. Number one on the list. A woman. An opera singer. An address. A house. *La Boulaye*. An opera singer. A voice. A beautiful woman. He started enquiring in the brothel. Naive, innocent questions.

'Where is the Opera?'

'Where do the singers live?'

They laughed at him, but he did not let that bother him. He fantasized about the singer. He imagined indistinct yet perfect features; he heard the sound of a fine voice. He continued to walk in the city as often as he could. What irritated him were the crowds, seeming to flow and coalesce in one great amorphous mass. He found the constant streams of bodies and faces overpowering. He began to believe there must an inherent destructive force in crowds, and that so many people should never be allowed to gather in one place.

The brothel had the same effect on him. The house was full of women, women's things, women's talk, women's smells. At the beginning he had liked the aroma of perfume, the girls' uninhibited chatter, the laced corsets and deep décolletés, the powdered wigs; but after a while these things lost some of their glitter, and he was no longer able to differentiate one body from another. The whole brothel lacked style or distinction, it seemed to him now. When he plucked the lice from Alphonse's head he had an overwhelming desire to strangle him. When he combed the girls' greasy hair or powdered their stinking wigs, he imagined himself shaving them all bald.

He could not sleep. Got up. Night of shadows. Outside: the city, that never stopped staring. Inside: the winding corridors. Noises from a room. The mechanical rhythm of mucous membranes. The smell of unwashed penis, the oil the girls smeared on their pink slits. Their lips exhausted from their work. Went along the twisting corridors, body tense. Opened the door of Valérie's room and lay down on her. Really erect. Penis pressed against her navel. Her soft belly wet with his semen the second before she woke. Ah! He scurried off in shame along the labyrinthine corridors. Fell asleep with her slap still resounding in his ears. No dreams.

At dawn the next day Latour left the brothel. As he stepped out of the doorway of 'The Last Resort' on to the Place de Grève he intended never to return. He made his way to the clump of trees where he had buried his share of Goupils' hoard, and filled his pockets. He took the treasure to a Jewish merchant in a building behind the Palais-Royal. As he was negotiating with him he suddenly felt afraid of being caught, and his legs began to tremble. He signed for the money in Goupils' name. His hand was wet with perspiration.

Emerging on to the street he thought, 'If there's a just God, He ought to strike me down now.'

He stood still and waited.

'Come on, God, smite me to the ground.'

Nothing happened. Latour gazed up at the sky. It looked different in Paris. Like an accusing face.

He walked towards the city centre along fashionable streets. His body felt calmer and he was no longer shaking, even though his hands were still unsteady. He clasped them in front of him. Now no one could doubt his composure.

'What is destruction?' he asked himself. 'Wasn't it the ancient Romans who said that everything was in a process of eternal flux? *Sub specie æternitatis* death is just a little push. A murder is nothing but a service to nature. A service that strong people perform for Mother Nature, simply because they are strong. For strong people destruction is a pleasure. The pain of others gives life meaning. That's how things are.'

He walked on.

Knee-breeches of black silk. A taffeta cloak with ruched armholes. Shoes with buckles. A wig. A tricorn hat. He was in a gentlemen's tailor's in the Rue Saint-Honoré, imagining himself with the whole world at his feet.

He is a nobleman. He has a chateau in Provence and a lover in Paris. They meet in the Jardin du Luxembourg. Swans. Crimson sun. He takes her to a room where lavender water cascades from marble fountains into bowls shaped like shells. She lies down for him on a divan. He fastens a white cloth over her eyes and draws an image of the Devil on her genitals.

Surrounded by looking-glasses and attentive salesmen, Latour was a gentleman, a person of authority and breeding, the person he had yearned to be ever since he was a child. The silk of his breeches was cool against his skin; he adjusted them and admired himself again in the glass. He drew the cloak around him and paid for the clothes rather stiffly. He strutted out of the door with impressive gait. The time had come to call at some of the city's better houses of pleasure.

'I am Comte Latour,' he said.

The madam of the brothel looked at him quizzically and responded with a smirk. Latour was not entirely sure whether it was a sign of mockery or of excessive respect. His gaze tarried on her neck and breasts, the delicate pink skin of a mature woman. He felt a tingle in his loins.

'The girls are at your disposal . . . Monsieur . . . le Comte. It is an honour to have you visit our establishment at last. I hope you will enjoy your experience with us.'

He climbed a staircase, traversed corridors that smelt of nutmeg, hurried impatiently across to a half-open door. There were three women waiting in the room.

Latour felt like a little god. He asked them to lie on the bed and not to move. They did as he requested. He caressed their bodies, slapped their rumps, felt their muscles and joints and knuckles and drew on them with a sharp quill pen. The girls shrieked. He ordered them to lie completely silent on the wide bed while he pinched them carefully on the buttocks. Little red marks appeared on the curvaceous hemispheres of flesh. He pinched as gently as he could: did you feel *that*, did *that* hurt, what about *this*?

Finally he bent over the most buxom one and entered her from behind. It was the first time he had actually had sexual intercourse, and it was soon over. He lay with his face buried in the hollow of her neck and pressed up against her comforting warmth, her soft body. She smelt of humankind, he thought, of fear and joy, but then he realized that she smelt of the lust of others, of his. When he raised his head, he was drenched in sweat.

Julie, lying beneath his perspiring body, was a healthy, clever twenty-five-year-old. She looked up into his wide eyes and thought he was as innocent as Peter of Hanover, the boy who had been found naked in a forest, who had never seen another human being and could not talk . . . 'Perhaps he's green enough to let me take him to Hercule tonight. Julie, you ought to be

Minister of Finance,' she bragged to herself, looking up at him tenderly.

An hour later Julie and Latour were strolling together along the Rue de Venise. Latour was happy. He was numb with physical contentment, thinking peaceful thoughts and suspecting no danger until he saw that the street ended in a graveyard. Suddenly Julie let go his arm and whistled into the darkness. He looked at her and saw that her face was quite expressionless, no smile or flirtatious eyes any more. He stood there waiting, smiling at her. A figure came towards him, club in hand. Latour made no attempt to move.

When the club struck him on the side of the head with a dull thud and he lost consciousness, he just had time to think, 'You don't deserve to live.'

*

He came to in the dim recesses beneath the Pont Neuf. He was lying amongst beggars, between mounds of silt. He opened his eyes cautiously, letting the daylight filter through his lashes. He had no wish to find out where he was or who was concealed under the filthy blankets around him. He closed his eyes again. He could see desert, a burning hot barren desert. He felt a distinct lightness in the head where the blow had fallen. A wind in the head that made him giddy, a discomforting sensation of nausea. He eventually sat up and began rocking back and forth to counteract the giddiness and drive out the image of sand. He thought, 'I am Latour,' and in that same instant it occurred to him that no one would have noticed if he had disappeared from the face of the earth. It was of no consequence whether he was called Latour, Philippe or Armande, because there was no one who knew who he was. He was no more than a physical presence with a shadow.

He wandered around Paris as a nobody. He looked neither up nor down, just straight ahead, towards an invisible point in the distance. He ate fruit and vegetables that he scavenged off the ground after the market had closed, he drank rainwater and he slept in sheltered corners under bridges. He did not speak to anyone and turned away whenever anyone tried to speak to him. He never slept two nights in the same place and rarely knew what street he was in. He saw processions, a dead horse, the play of shadows on a wall, a pale woman in a sedan chair, the sunset reflected in the Seine. He walked. Walked and walked. In the mornings the streets were slippery after the rain in the night. In the middle of the day he was aware of the strong odour of human beings.

One evening he followed two beautiful noblewomen. They were sitting in an open carriage, and Latour ran along beside it, captivated by their pale, almost ethereal faces. They alighted outside a large building, which several hundred people were entering. He stopped to listen to the murmur of voices, the laughter, the sense of expectation in the air. After a while it all quietened down. He went nearer. He heard a voice from within, a woman's voice, singing in a way he would not have thought possible. The exquisite sound almost pierced his eardrums. He stood there thinking about the woman who was singing. An opera. An opera singer. He thought of the multiplicity of feelings her face would be able to express.

He envisaged the city as a huge body cut open: bones, joints, blood vessels exposed, a woman's body, and himself walking around inside it. To begin with he felt excited, a feeling of power, but then the image became fuzzy and seemed to slip through his fingers, the body evaporating into the streets.

The city itself became fuzzy, everything dissolving into everything else. He would wake at night to an awareness, just as on that first night beneath the Pont Neuf, that he was Latour. But now it was an effort to answer the question of what his name was.

*

In the Rue des Deux-Ecus he heard her voice again. As he crawled under a gate into a dark overgrown garden, the singing from the brightly lit room above sounded to him like the wailing of some unknown animal. It had not been difficult to find her, and as he followed the path towards her voice he felt cool and clear-headed. He stood now by the espaliers staring up at her room through the foliage of the fruit trees. He could not see anyone, but felt as if he were standing close by her. A gentle breeze fanned his face and the scent of artichokes and strawberries wafted over him. He listened to the singing practice, the vowels gliding into each other and forming musical motifs in the air. The beautiful voice made him uneasy. And then fearful. He tore himself away from the wall and cautiously approached the house. He saw a silhouette, and then the singer herself appeared at the window and stood motionless looking straight out into the dark garden. *La Boulaye*. She was wearing a gown of silk and pricked muslin, a sumptuous creation. Latour backed away, surprised to see her suddenly there above him looking completely different from the picture he had formed in his mind. He turned and ran for the gate as fast as he could. He heard her voice behind him, 'Eduardo?'

The next night he was in the garden again. The scene was repeated. He stood by the fruit trees, and she sang in her room above, invisible to him. There was someone with her, but an hour later he saw a man leave the house. So now she was alone. He had thought about her face, her wig and her shimmering gown. He had thought of her long neck and the sound that emanated from it, he had thought of her throat, of her contor-

tions as he cut out her larynx. When she at last stopped singing and sat at the piano instead to play dance music, he began
to tremble. He went over towards the open window.

He climbed up on to the balcony. Only when his bare feet
were touching the stone floor did he become aware of how
loud the piano was, the sound rolling through the room like
waves and pouring over him. He felt like dancing, though he
did not know how. He leaned forward warily to look into the
room. She was seated at the piano playing with her eyes closed.
Her smile crept a little higher up her left cheek than the right.
A delicate crease at the corner of her mouth. Pale pink powder.
She did not react to his presence until she felt his hand on her
throat. That was the moment he saw her first contortion.

He cleaned the scalpel in a barrel of water some distance away.
He dug a hole in the ground with his fingers to bury his blood-
stained shirt. Then he drew out the little piece of bone shaped
like an apricot kernel and rinsed that too in the barrel before
returning it to his pocket.

He felt like a king.

As he emerged from the courtyard to make his way towards
the Pont Neuf, he caught sight of two police constables, walking along together engaged in animated conversation. In front
of them was a crippled Spaniard with a crutch. Latour moved
off calmly in the opposite direction, and then heard the
Spaniard's excited cry.

'That's him! That's him! The man in the long cloak!'

Latour started running, bounding up the street and into a
narrow side alley overhung by trees. He could hear the police-
men's voices behind him, angry shouts, boots clattering on the
paving stones. He ran along by a low wall until he saw the
lights of the main road. He stopped, swung round and watched

the three men heading towards him. When they saw that he had come to a halt they slowed down. Latour glanced up at the sky for a moment. It was dark blue, with thin wisps of yellowy cloud in the shape of a fan. He listened to their footsteps and imagined he could even hear their breathing. Something in him wanted simply to stand there and wait for the blows. The Spaniard's shout brought him to his senses.

'Grab him!'

He threw himself over the wall and ran in zig-zags between the ornamental shrubs in the dark garden. He clambered over one fence and then another. He opened a door and came out on to a boulevard. The voices of his pursuers had grown fainter, almost inaudible.

He crept behind a carriage in which the coachman was half asleep and squeezed up against the big wet wheel; as voices approached he crawled round on to the axle. Suddenly the doors banged to and the coach jerked into motion with the crack of a whip. He held on tight to the axle as they drove in and out of back streets and jolted across open squares. He could hear two men talking within about the murder that had just been committed on an opera singer. One of them had once heard La Boulaye perform, and Latour felt quite touched when he heard his description of her singing.

At a bend in the road the carriage skidded on the slippery mud. The horse shied. The axle snapped. The wheels span. Latour was catapulted to the ground.

*

The Hôtel-Dieu hospital was one of the most ancient in Europe. Founded in 660 by the Bishop of Paris, its external appearance inspired veneration, with rows of high windows flanking its Grecian columns. But internally the building suffered from unhygienic conditions, inadequate equipment and overcrowding. It stank. There were twelve hundred beds, often with four patients to each and a high mortality rate, the smell of every imminent death clearly discernible in the surrounding streets. Tenon, the famous surgeon, was later to call the Hôtel-Dieu 'the most insalubrious and unwelcoming hospital in existence'.

A young student, Charles Cantin, walked pensively through the crowded wards, no longer paying any attention to the patients around him, ignoring their moans and groans. Charles had come from Cherbourg three months earlier to study surgery and anatomy under a surgeon who was an old acquaintance of his father. But his conscience was beginning to trouble him. The Hôtel-Dieu made him feel ill. He could not tolerate the stench and the appalling conditions. He had come to Paris to study anatomy, to become a great anatomist, not to sew corpses into sacks. Now he had to ponder the question of whether to follow his father's wishes and carry on studying under this uninspiring surgeon, or whether to apply for a place to study with the disgraced anatomist Rouchefoucault. He met another young man in the corridor, his friend Jean-Georges, who accompanied him through the lofty rooms and out into the evening sunset. They sat on the wall outside to discuss the difficult choice confronting Charles. Jean-Georges called Rouchefoucault a charlatan.

'He was expelled from the Collège Royal. He gets up to the strangest things, Charles. You'd saddle yourself with a very bad reputation if you worked with him.'

'He's the best anatomist in the city.'

'Not everyone would agree.'

'I've watched him myself doing dissections in the Anatomy Theatre. He really is the best.'

'It's your father's wish that you study here.'

'But what if my father's wish isn't the right thing for me?'

106

The pair were so engrossed in this moral dilemma that they failed to observe the hunched figure sitting on the wall beside them, nor did they see it gradually straighten up as the argument became more heated.

It was dusk when Charles left the grand white building to go to Professor Rouchefoucault and ask to be taken on as his student, against the advice of his friend Jean-Georges. As he came out of the hospital grounds he was so preoccupied with his decision that he was unaware of the shadowy figure pursuing him. Crossing the Île de la Cité bridge he began to have an uncomfortable feeling of being followed, but it was only as he took a short cut through the alley leading to the Rue des Mathurins that he caught sight of the diminutive creature and stopped.

'Excuse me, Monsieur, I'm trying to find a particular address.'

The man's voice was quaking; he seemed nervous. Charles looked at his outstretched hand and hesitated. His wrinkled face and tattered cloak did not inspire confidence. It reminded him of the atmosphere of the Hôtel-Dieu, something which he was only too keen to put behind him.

'I can't work out which way to go,' the man croaked.

To Charles there was something helpless and pitiful about the fellow; he seemed innocuous enough. Inwardly amused by his own apprehensiveness he went nearer, to explain that he did not know the city very well.

'I've only lived in Paris for three months myself.'

Craning forward to read the address on the piece of paper Charles noticed that the man smelt of salt, momentarily recalling Cherbourg and his mother, father and sister, the ships, the fish and the salt warehouses. He scanned the sheet the man was holding — it was blank. As he opened his mouth to point this out he caught sight of the stone in the other hand lunging towards him, a fraction of a second before he felt the cold blow against his temple. What a ridiculous remark to make, he thought, as he teetered in front of the stranger, staring in amazement into his blue eyes before falling to the ground. His last conscious perception was of the man removing the papers from his coat pocket.

As night descended on the city, enveloping the Pont Petit and Île de la Cité in blackness, Latour dragged the student's naked body down to the river bank and tossed it into the water.

The next morning he was knocking at Rouchefoucault's door. How did he come to be here? He had been living as a beggar. And now he had beaten a man to death, stolen his clothes and documents. He was perfectly cognisant of the facts of the situation, he could visualize every detail of what had happened. The young student's subtle perfume still lingered in his nostrils. But the act had something involuntary and inevitable about it, almost as if it had not been his own hand that had carried it out. No, not the hand of another person so much as another part of himself that had done the deed. The downcast beggar had given way to the fanatic. His mind dwelt joyously on his own strength and decisiveness. On the doorstep he hugged himself as if he were freezing, and chuckled. Then he knocked on the door again.

Rouchefoucault was leaning over the dissecting table when his servant announced the unexpected visitor. The anatomist gave a grunt of annoyance. He hated being interrupted. He disliked the unforeseen, the unplanned, the inconvenient. He knew that people in general accepted the nuisance of chance events as an inevitable aspect of daily life, and that tolerance was regarded as modern. But he had no time for such things. He was too busy. His life was organized down to the last detail: working time, meal times, reading, drawing, note-taking and dissection. He had given up his lectures because they constantly brought unpredictable vexations. He had left it to his colleague Hoffmann to take on the task of spreading the knowledge of his work. Hoffmann was a Dane who had turned himself into a Frenchman, a gentle character of enthusiastic temperament who obviously liked 'floating in space' as the Jansenists would say. Hoffmann loved the unpredictable. Rouchefoucault just felt increasingly grateful that that part of his work had been taken off his shoulders.

He turned now and inspected the intruder with scarcely veiled animosity. The young man before him was trembling with either excitement or nervousness. His hands, his whole body shook. His wrinkled old-man's face was positively vibrating.

'My name is Charles Cantin,' Latour mumbled.

'What do you want?'

Rouchefoucault was already impatient.

'I . . . I . . . I . . . would like to be your pupil.'

Rouchefoucault gave a snort.

'Are you the one who wrote to me?'

'That's correct, Monsieur.'

'You've been studying at the Hôtel-Dieu?'

'Anatomy and surgery, Monsieur. I . . .'

'Have you any idea what kind of things I do?'

'I've seen you dissecting in the Anatomy Theatre. You're the best in the country.'

Rouchefoucault made a gesture to interrupt him.

'Don't stand there talking nonsense!' he said with a twitch of irritation.

Latour glanced down at himself, at the student's knee-breeches and the polished shoes that were somewhat too big, at his ruched sleeves that reminded him of mesembryan-themums. For a moment it was as if time stood still. Then a spasm went through his body, and he straightened up and looked the anatomist in the eyes.

'Ask me any question you like about anatomy, Monsieur. Try me. I know everything.'

Rouchefoucault's eyes and curt guffaw betrayed his exasperation, and he was about to dismiss the boy without further ado when a devilish instinct decided him to expose Latour's arrogance and humiliate him before letting him slink away. He would contrive a really difficult question. He crossed his arms over his broad chest and looked down condescendingly on the trembling figure before him.

'What lies between the lateral hemisphere and the temporal lobe?' he asked with a faint sneer. It was a trick question because there was nothing between the two.

'The aqueduct of Sylvius.'

Latour almost spat it out. Rouchefoucault tightened his arms across his chest. The boy was obviously cleverer than he appeared at first sight, because it was true enough that the aqueduct of Sylvius went diagonally upwards from the temporal lobe. He decided to get down to more detail, intent upon humiliating him and determined to do so without being unscientific.

'What does the white matter of the brain consist of?'

Latour stood motionless, his forehead creased in concentration. Rouchefoucault was gratified to see his puzzled expression. But then Latour looked him in the eye again.

'It was once thought that it contained animal spirit, but Vieussens showed that it was composed of bunches of multitudinous intertwined fibres. The structure is revealed clearly when cooked in oil . . .'

Rouchefoucault studied his protruding blue eyes, his intense gaze. This Charles Cantin must have read both Vesalius and Raymond de Vieussens, which was far from usual among students of anatomy.

'What is the best way to open the brain?'

He smiled to himself. He knew that the medical schools still

110

taught Vesalius' inept method of starting the operation from the top. He would take the opportunity to strike a blow at this old heresy and then throw the student out, as a living example of the inadequacy of established medicine.

'It was formerly done from the top. Vieussens did it from the base.'

Rouchefoucault ceased his questioning. He looked down at his hands as if seeking an answer there. He had not managed to send the boy packing, and it occurred to him that he was acting against his own best interests. He had been wanting an assistant with a good knowledge of anatomy for some time. This lad standing before him had a rather offputting external appearance, gnomelike and intense, but otherwise there seemed to be little against him. He had even managed to answer quite complex questions. He regarded him with renewed interest, not least his protruberant eyes.

'Come back in the morning,' he said, attempting a smile. But realizing that it looked forced, he turned quickly and went off to his dissecting room without further ado. Latour took a few hesitant steps after him, to express his gratitude, but before he could utter a word, Rouchefoucault had already disappeared.

Latour paused and cast his eyes over the high, light ceiling, the Chinese-pattern wallpaper, the arched passageway leading to the workrooms. He thought he could detect the faint odour of alcohol from the dissecting room. He closed his eyes with a sense of relief: he was now Charles Cantin, pupil of the great anatomist. He formed the shape of the new name on his tongue. Charles. Charles Cantin. It felt good.

It was early one summer's morning when Latour started work with the anatomist, and six months were to pass before he was again to walk the streets of Paris.

Rouchefoucault's working day began at sunrise and continued without interruption until lunch time. After a two-hour break he would resume his labours and seldom finish until after midnight. Latour never strayed more than a few yards from him throughout the whole day and evening. At night he slept in the maid's room behind Rouchefoucault's chamber and could hear him snoring. He became familiar with his insistence on precision, his shyness of strangers, his eating habits. He knew what angered him and what excited him. He realized that he was superstitious, and that there were certain things that should never be taken into the dissecting room.

Rouchefoucault's obstinacy was a byword among the Paris medical fraternity; Latour could actually see the stubbornness in his fingertips. His absorption in his task, eyes that never seemed to suffer from fatigue. As an anatomist Rouchefoucault was untiring, methodical. His anatomical theories might sound fanciful, but he himself was cautious in the extreme and of a sensitive and introverted disposition. He was sure that his theories about the organs of the brain were correct and revolutionary. He took the time to explain his remarkable cranial theory to Latour, leaning forward to address him and gesticulating passionately.

The brain had been regarded as the seat of the soul ever since Greek antiquity. Galen gave an exact description of the functions of the chambers of the brain and posited their connection with intellectual functions such as the imagination, reason, memory. The Church Fathers localized these faculties to particular organs of the brain and developed what was called the doctrine of cells. All these beliefs were later rejected. Rouchefoucault had almost ruined his sight poring over tomes of mediæval medicine, studying the old anatomical illustrations until he had got spots before his eyes. His sensational cranial theory was based on the assumption that mental faculties could be read from the surface of the brain. The topography of the skull, with its bumps and hollows, provided a map of the conjunctions in the brain beneath. Rouchefoucault could ascertain a lot about a person by simply studying the shape of the head. By feeling the skull with his fingertips and by taking measurements with specially designed instruments he could determine personal characteristics and their qualities.

'I was ten years old when I realized that people with protruding eyes often have extremely good memories,' he said, clasping his hands. 'Later I discovered that the anterior convolutions of the frontal lobes are contiguous with the postero-lateral aspects of the eyeball.'

He grabbed Latour by the nape of the neck and pulled his startled assistant towards him.

'You can feel it here.'

He pressed his fingers into Latour's forehead.

'When these brain convolutions are well developed, this part of the sphenoid bone, which forms the posterior third of the exterior wall of the eye socket, is pushed forward. This diminishes the depth of the eye sockets and causes the eyes to protrude more than usual. Such people are endowed with a superb memory for words and are particularly well-suited to the study of language and literature. They collate information, write history and make excellent librarians.'

He released Latour's neck and the latter rubbed his eyes. He had been taunted at school for having ferrety eyes — they had always been slightly protruberant. Rouchefoucault took him by the arm and led him over to a wall of the dissecting room where there hung a row of diagrams, anatomical drawings of the human head with personal faculties marked. Rouchefoucault stood for a moment admiring his own expertise. When he spoke again it was in an almost affectionate tone of voice.

'I thought, why should other faculties not have their own overt characteristics? I have dissected five hundred brains over the last ten years, Charles, and identified nineteen different faculties on the surface of the brain.'

He pointed at the diagrams.

1. Love of progeny. 2. Self-defence and courage. 3. Cunning, ingenuity. 4. Possessiveness, greed, dishonesty. 5. Pride, arrogance, self-importance, love of authority. 6. Vanity, ambition, love of glory. 7. Prudence, caution. 8. Memory. 9. Linguistic ability. 10. Sense of colour, sound and music. 11. Wisdom, sense of metaphysics. 12. Satire, wit. 13. Poetic talent. 14. Sense of pain. 15. Kindness, sympathy. 16. Mimicry. 17. Religious sentiment. 18. Decisiveness, singleness of purpose. 19. Morality.

Latour looked in wonder from the anatomist to the map of the brain.

'Of these I have found nine corresponding organs. What we are seeking to achieve now, young man, is a comprehensive chart of such correspondences, and then my theory will be published and conquer the world. Come, let's get to work.'

＊

Latour sat at the open window with his eyes closed, while the anatomist slept in the inner chamber. Even against the noise of the city outside he could hear his snores. He was considering the events of the last few days in the dissecting room. He thought of how the brain was dissected, like a mysterious fruit opening, the wet, grey mass. It resembled a walnut. A spider's web. The folds of the gyri. The complex patterns of the convolutions and cavities. The aqueduct of Sylvius. Grey and white matter. Nerve fibres. Latour had felt infinitely small when Rouchefoucault had expertly pulled down the flaps of skin over the face of the corpse and exposed the skull. And as he continued the dissection, opening up the brain from the underside, in accordance with Vieussens' method, it struck Latour that Rouchefoucault's mastery was consummate.

Latour admired Rouchefoucault immensely. Everything the man did was magical. Latour wrote up the notes on the dissections and often found himself holding the pen so tight that it snapped. Rouchefoucault did not have any advanced instruments but on the contrary prided himself on using only the simplest. Scissors, tweezers, various scalpels, a hammer, a bone saw for the skull and a sharp pair of forceps. His method was not to cut but to follow the nerve fibres. He would scrape his way through the brain matter without damaging the fibres. He had excellent sight and maintained that he could see them with his naked eye.

He thought he had located the organ connected with cunning and ingenuity close to the cerebellum and was utterly convinced that the organs of mimicry and pain must be nearby. But dissection was difficult in that area. Latour was entranced. He was intoxicated. Rouchefoucault was a genius. But Latour never betrayed his exhilaration; in fact he never said much at all, just watching the anatomist with eyes that seemed to burn right through his pale-coloured gown. Latour worked quickly, gradually developing the ability to anticipate what Rouchefoucault would request. He would frequently proffer the instrument before Rouchefoucault had managed to form the words.

When the corpses lay on the dissecting bench in front of him, Latour felt a profound sense of excitement. The two of them had complete control. He would stoop over the lifeless heads, knowing that soon the flesh would be loosened from the cranium, and the facial characteristics erased. They all looked equally ugly on the dissecting bench. The bodies lay there with their brains cut into slices, their skin peeled back over their faces. The pain in this room was as detached as in a work of art; it belonged to no one. There was total silence here, broken only by the tinkle of instruments. It satisfied Latour, but he did not think that Rouchefoucault felt the same. The anatomist was indifferent to the bodies, they were simply dead matter on which he happened to be performing research. But for Latour the dead were conveyors of a private bond.

Rouchefoucault had lived his life for anatomy, dissecting animals since he was thirteen, and made great demands for self-sacrifice on Latour's part. But not once in all the time Latour served as his apprentice did he have cause for complaint. This strangely stooped young man was the most diligent and talented pupil he had ever had.

But Latour suspected the idyll could not last, and the end, when it came, arose from human inquisitiveness. When Hoffman started working with Rouchefoucault again and was preparing a series of lectures about their recent discoveries, he was so impressed with Latour that he decided to check on the background of this Charles Cantin.

Latour was washing in the dissecting room when the servant announced that there was an inspector from the Hôtel-Dieu at the door. Rouchefoucault gave his usual grunt of irritation, put down his scalpel and forceps in a bowl of water and went out to receive him. Latour stood listening to the voices emanating from the hall. He had often thought this situation could arise sooner or later and had imagined what might be said: the initial enquiries about the student's name, the scepticism in the tone of voice, Rouchefoucault's brusque dismissal, the inspector's insistence, a brief discussion and then . . . then they came walking along the corridor towards the dissecting room. Latour slipped out unseen through the kitchen and the back yard on to the street, where he melted into the flow of people.

He put a good distance between himself and Rouchefoucault's house and wandered aimlessly around the streets by the old city wall. He tried not to think about what Rouchefoucault must now know. That he was a fraud. A criminal! The thought of the anatomist's disappointed face drove him to a fury of despair. He crept furtively along like a thief, pulling his cloak over his head. At nightfall he slept in the bushes without even covering himself, waking to find his hands blue with frost. All he wanted was to close his eyes and carry on walking until he fell into the Seine. So on he went, concealed in his cloak, colliding with carriages, people, walls, bleeding from a cut on the forehead but ignoring it, people shouting at him, shoving him, just walking resolutely on. Towards the Seine.

In the Place de Grève he bumped into a woman. A familiar voice. Valérie was shaking him, slapping him round the face. But he felt nothing. He closed his eyes again. She hissed his name, and he fell down on his knees before her and stuttered unintelligibly, 'I'm sorry . . . , I'm sorry . . .'

She took him back to the brothel and looked after him. When he came to he found himself lying in a large bed beneath a scarlet quilt. He looked up at Valérie's motherly figure and felt a stab of that same tenderness for her that he had once felt in Honfleur.

*

Latour went on working in the brothel as if nothing had happened. He told no one that he had been studying under the famous anatomist. But Rouchefoucault and the dissecting room would often come into his mind. He would lie there musing about theories as if he were still the anatomist's apprentice. He dreamt about corpses. He speculated about the organs of the brain that had still not been identified and about the sense of pain.

117

Then his thoughts turned again to his list and the bodies. He would pause in the middle of a task, a far-away expression on his face, deaf and blind to the whole world. What actually was it that was circling round in his head, that he could not put into words? Was it the pain of the victims? Or what Latour himself felt when he saw their pain? An inner emotion, a secret ecstasy. It was frightening because he felt it might drive him away, away from himself. He imagined he could see people before him, in their wigs and cloaks, in their muslins and frockcoats. He could see their individual anatomical features. He imagined he saw the pain in their faces as he cut them open. He fantasized in detail on how he would dissect their brains.

In a medical bookshop in Montmartre he came upon Hoffmann's pamphlets on cranial theory for the general public. He sat in the Jardin du Luxembourg and read them from cover to cover. When he stood up he was seething with anger. Hoffmann presented the theory as if it were the result of cooperation between himself and Rouchefoucault; and it was badly described, a parody of the master's meticulous precision. Latour threw the pamphlets down in disgust and left the park, walking the streets from district to district and heading unconsciously towards Rouchefoucault's house. When he realized this he flushed, pulled his cloak up round his ears and hurried home.

He used to spy on the girls. He would often sit in Valérie's cupboard, squashed in between her heavy gowns, his eyes glued to a crack in the door. But he could see very little from that angle, only the white wall and the shadows of figures on the bed. He watched their movements and heard Valérie's feigned squeals of delight. The man's heavy breathing. Laughter. Moans. Commands, pleading. He felt there was something else he needed to make sense of the shadows on the wall and the noises and the movements. Yet he still sat as often as he could in Valérie's cupboard, watching the shadows.

One day he was on the staircase, nailing a broken tread, when a nobleman came over to him. Short in stature with a high forehead and intense eyes, he raised his hat and gave Latour a beaming smile without saying a word. Latour looked up at his blue eyes, taking in his broad face and the fine cloak thrown over his shoulder. He didn't know him. One of the girls passed them, jumping over the step, but the man took no notice of her, just grinned sarcastically. Latour had the impression he might at any moment burst into laughter or utter an obscenity.

'I'd like to offer you a job,' he said suddenly. He had a pleasing, cultivated, voice.

Latour looked at him uncomprehendingly.

'I need a valet.'

'What?'

'I can show you the only sensible way to live.'

'I don't understand.'

'Libertinism.'

'Monsieur, I think you should talk to Madame,' said Latour, turning away to concentrate on hammer, nail and stair. But the stranger did not move.

'Latour!'

The voice stung his ear, and he tried to conceal his annoyance.

'Do you know me?'

'I've had you in my sights for several weeks.'

'Monsieur, I don't wish to appear lacking in respect but I have a lot to do, so if you've finished with your joke I would like to get on with repairing this step.'

The nobleman nodded condescendingly.

'You came here with Valérie. You have an observant eye.' He leaned forward and whispered, almost ironically, 'I can teach you all about pleasure.'

Latour looked at him in some confusion. It *must* be a joke.

'Why have you come to me, Monsieur?'

'You are the ugliest man I have ever seen. I like that. I like your insolent expression. I've seen you lurking around the corridors here. Don't think I don't know you're a cheeky little devil. They don't call you the Parrot for nothing. You could be of use to me.'

Latour no longer knew what to say. He rose and moved back up the stairs. The nobleman grinned, his smile almost a grimace.

'I'll come and fetch you soon, my boy.'

Latour heard him still laughing as he went off. The girls in the salon turned to stare at them.

Two months passed without any sign of the nobleman.

Latour was bored. He started rummaging through Valérie's room whenever she was out, whiling away an hour or so rooting around among her corsets and erotic aids. One morning he came across a notebook in her drawer. Its pages were filled with dense handwriting, but it was not Valérie's. He sat down on the side of the bed to peruse it.

A young and virtuous woman became lost in a dense forest. She was attacked by robbers. The next morning she was found by a group of monks. She besought these holy men to take her with them to their monastery. They assented. The young woman thanked them, wept, repeated her thanks. But once there she was subjected to the monks' shockingly unbridled lust. She was bound and tortured. They whipped her breasts and raped her in a way that left her virtue intact. Yet she never gave up her belief in innocence, even though she herself met with nothing but cruelty, perversion and indifference.

Paris was flooded with erotic tales; they were an inflationary commodity. But Latour had nothing better to do, so he read the whole story. It had a certain style; the author could write well. After a few pages Latour was gripped by it and he suddenly discovered that he had been sitting on the edge of Valérie's bed reading for several hours. Dusk was falling; he could hear the costermongers pulling their barrows along the street and the voices of the girls from the salon: the first clients had already arrived.

> I learnt the cruel lesson that if there are people motivated by hatred or shameful lust who can take delight in the pain of others, there are also those creatures who are barbaric enough to find the same pleasure for no other reason than arrogance or inhuman curiosity . . .

The tale was unfinished, to his great frustration. He hunted through Valérie's drawers and cupboards but could find no more pages. Who had placed it in her drawer? A client? Why? Was it a game, a sex aid? He put the notebook away and decided to try and forget it. But a few days later he remembered the story and the young woman's fear again and went back to Valérie's room to re-read it. But the notebook was gone. He searched the whole room, to no avail. Instead a disturbing image came into his mind: a vision of the singer, lying at his feet on the floor of her bedroom, himself standing over her, scalpel in hand. It was so clear that he was filled again with the sensation of power and freedom. Whenever he thought he had succeeded in ridding himself of the image and could relax, it would reappear. It tormented him for several days and even made him feel ill.

To divert his mind he began hiding in Valérie's cupboard again, to watch the shadows and listen to the voices.

'Strike me with your glove, Mademoiselle. Harder. There. That's right. A bit harder. Lower down, lower down . . .'

A man's voice.

'Roll over, my dearest. What exquisite globes! I'm going to

transform these white fruits into lush crimson temptations.'

Whip crack. Whip crack. Latour could imagine hearing the sound of flesh reddening.

The man embarked on a long discourse.

'What a sweet little hole, my kitten. Let me kiss it. Let me bite it . . . Some women put sponges in their vagina . . . Venetian leather . . . condoms . . . to stop the semen . . . and . . . prevent the creation of further generations . . . a praiseworthy undertaking . . . But of all preventive measures . . . I prefer . . . without a doubt . . . the one represented . . . by the anus . . . Let us devote ourselves . . . to this piquant delight . . . Ah! a divine fuck, what a tight little thing.'

And:

'Punish me.'

Whip crack. Whip crack.

Latour tried to rise to his knees in the cupboard but in doing so lost his balance and fell against the door and through it, landing on the floor beside the bed. The man who was talking lay on the bed with a stole of lynx fur across his shoulders. Valérie was standing over him with a cat-o'-nine-tails in her hand. They didn't even notice him: it was as if they had eyes and ears only for each other. Latour sat motionless on the floor. He felt infinitely small. Excluded, superfluous. As the ritual continued, and the man went on with his commentary, which in the circumstances seemed absurd, Latour crawled across the floor to hide under the bed. New commands, screams of delight. He saw the whip descending on Valérie's body and heard the man extolling her ugly face. He heard her frenzied panting, her sexual arousal in the dimly lit room. When it was all over, they embraced. She stroked his face, kissed his cheeks.

'I haven't any money,' the man said. 'I'll have to borrow some more; I'll ask my uncle.'

Valérie said nothing.

'I'll be back in the morning.'

As he went to the door, Latour caught a glimpse of his face. It was the stocky nobleman who had offered him a job.

After that Latour felt embarrassed whenever he met Valérie's eyes and he had a feeling that she was aware he knew her more intimately than was his right.

Nevertheless he was in the cupboard again the following evening. He found it difficult to sit still. A sequence of clients, but no sign of the nobleman. He sat in the cupboard every night for some weeks before the latter reappeared. New rituals were enacted. The nobleman screamed ecstatically as if he were *in extremis*. Once more they stood holding each other afterwards for an eternity. As he was about to go, again confessing to having no money, Valérie whispered sympathetically — and used his name.

Donatien Alphonse François de Sade.

Unnoticed, Latour slipped out of the room and followed him.

Born into the nobility. Related to the Abbot of Samane. Military career. Royal consent to his engagement. The talk of Paris. Stories and more stories. About blasphemy. Perversions, cruelty. Inspector Marais had asked the brothels of Paris not to serve him. The old Jeanne Testard affair. Slender Jeanne from Madame du Rameau's brothel in the Rue Saint Honoré. The long drive through the dark streets of the Faubourg St Marceau. He had enticed her into a house, down into a cellar, and questioned her about her religious beliefs, shouting blasphemies at her. On the walls: erotic pictures, a cross, whips with metal points. There were detailed rumours. He asked whether she liked . . . terrible things: enemas, whipping, sodomy. She implored him to spare her life. He was committed to Vincennes prison later that autumn. But by the spring he was back in the brothels, nothing had changed. He was living a dissolute life on borrowed money, creating scandals in the brothels and infuriating the police and the guardians of morality.

Latour ran through the streets after the Marquis' carriage. He was dripping with sweat when he arrived at the house in the Rue Neuve du Luxembourg, between La Madeleine and the Jardin des Tuileries. As he followed him up the steps he muttered to himself, 'Marquis de Sade, I've come to throttle you.'

He pushed open the door and found himself standing in an ill-lit corridor, the man he was pursuing no longer in sight. He peered about him, took a few hesitant paces, listened but could hear nothing. As he edged stealthily forward he felt an arm round his throat, impossible to escape. The Marquis must have been waiting for him in the shadows.

'Monsieur . . . It's Latour. I've been thinking about your offer . . . If you need a good assistant, Monsieur . . . I'm more than willing . . . unreservedly . . . at your service, Monsieur . . .'

The Marquis did not answer, merely tightened his hold on Latour's neck. Latour tried to stand still. Everything went black before his eyes. Then just as he thought he was on the point of dying, the Marquis loosed his grip.

Two days later he fetched Latour from the brothel. Latour sat opposite him as the carriage flew through the streets of Paris. He studied the Marquis' blue eyes, his thin lips that were constantly in motion or being suddenly sucked in and disappearing from his face entirely. Latour's impression of having made a fool of himself gave way to a sense of fellow-feeling with the Marquis de Sade; he could imagine he was like him, that it was he, Latour, who was leaning forward, talking animatedly, smugly and derisively of abbots and judges. He noted the Marquis' patterns of speech, his movements, the posture of his stocky body, and mimicked it all in his mind, the way an actor studies a living model for a part he is about to play.

4

Latour's List

I leaned on the stone windowsill and looked out over our hosts' property. The sky had turned red. The sun had disappeared but left a crimson glow over Echauffour. I would soon be going to bed, to dream. About a young woman with a beautifully formed cranium, about the patterns within the brain.

I was back in Normandy, no more than a day's journey from Honfleur. All the way here through the dark forests the Marquis and I sat staring straight ahead at the road before us. At L'Aigle we turned north-west towards the Cotentin Peninsula. I recognized the old familiar smells. The Channel, salty yet cloyingly sweet, an odour of putrefaction, I thought: beneath that beguiling surface lay the corpses of a million sea-creatures. The woods, the scent of the apple orchards in blossom.

The Marquis had been advised to keep away from Paris. He was anxious to avoid Vincennes Prison; he could not bear to be incarcerated. Staying with his parents-in-law was punishment enough, he said. I thought of Monsieur de Montreuil, the Judge, Madame de Montreuil and their daughter Anne-Prosphère (of whom the Marquis always spoke most warmly) as characters from a fairy-tale. I realized that I was looking forward to our stay with the eager anticipation of a child, a mixture of curiosity and fear. These were worthy people, the fair-minded bourgeoisie who had not relied on the privileges of nobility to acquire their morality and elegance. Madame de Sade had journeyed on ahead to put everything in order for her husband and to prepare the family for his impossible temperament. My expectations were altogether too high.

The Montreuils' estate, including the house of simple white stone surrounded by fences, occupied the heights at the edge of the forest with views over the little country town below. On a clear day I could even see the hills of lower Normandy. The first night I felt as if I were suffocating, a very uncomfortable sensation. I rose from my bed and stood at the window staring out over fields and forest. I was as if transported back to Honfleur, standing in Bou-Bou's cottage watching a deer browsing among the trees.

I carried out my duties assiduously. The lady of the house was very strict, with a peremptory voice; she was a small and dispirited person, with an expressionless face. I had already seen through her. She was indifferent to the sufferings of others but demanded sympathy for her own infirmities, her spine, her hips, any slight headache: she had a new ailment every week. I thought she had fallen a little in love with her son-in-law, the 'chevalier'. She was always in his proximity, smiling; and he was very attentive to her, paying her compliments and flirting with her. Unfortunately I was not so sure it was merely a game: the Marquis was obviously interested.

She was totally obsessed with the family, this lady, with power, money, her daughters' merits. Yet she had closed herself off from the world, and she did not like the silence in her own head. There was a desperation in her voice, in her fingers as they clutched her wine glass to convey it to her lips, in her eyes as they followed the path of the sun over the town. She would have liked more power. When she was asleep she resembled a mummy; awake, her eyes were so sharp that I sometimes feared she knew my opinion of her.

I sat down at night and made a sketch of her head.

'The way you let your family treat you!'

'Have you no pride?'

'The least you could do is make yourself look more attractive.'

My master was a tyrant. He bullied his wife. But Madame de Sade did not complain. Renée was a good-natured woman and the more good-nature she showed, the more malicious he became, the more he enjoyed tormenting her, just a little, never too much. And she clung to these reproofs as others would to kindness. At every hour of the day she would wait for the stab, the spiteful barb that would confirm his love for her. She was melancholy and took delight in being so. He was the master of melancholy; in her dejected posture he saw a reflection of himself. But I knew what went on in her mind. All she wanted was to lay her head on her husband's chest and imagine their love to be a secret. I had an impulsive urge to hold Madame Renée myself, to stroke her head, but it was out of the question. Whenever I thought she must have had enough, that her face was about to dissolve into tears, he drew her close, stroked her playfully and whispered affectionate words in her ear.

'Divine pussycat, you mean everything to me.'

He had his eye on Madame Renée's younger sister now, Anne-Prosphère, and Renée was buzzing around that potential dalliance like a bee about a honeypot. Anne-Prosphère was spoilt and just as conceited as her mother. But pretty. And beside her elder sister she looked even prettier. I had determined not to like her but I could not resist covertly studying the shape of her body and her skull. I stood and stared at her as if from afar. I stood in the Marquis' old coat and worn-out boots and stared.

I sat down at night and made a sketch of Anne-Prosphère's head.

The Marquis' amusements here were flirting with Madame, teasing the wretched Judge, tormenting Renée. Apart from that he was content to adhere to the rules like anyone else. Madame de Montreuil would tolerate no irregularities. So the Marquis changed for dinner, comported himself well at table, praised Madame's wit, her good taste and so forth. He accompanied them to church, did not mock God nor rage against religion. He exuded charm. Everything was done correctly. As befitted a worthy family.

They had all this: grand rooms, boudoirs, fine furnishings, Chinese vases, bathrooms that smelt of lily of the valley.

But where was the happiness?

The happiness was mine.

*

I helped the Marquis unpack the books he had brought with him for his stay, two trunks full. As we arranged them in careful alphabetical sequence on the shelves, I could tell that something was distracting him. It was early in the morning and raining heavily outside; the sound of the rain enveloped us and made everything seem very peaceful. There was a bluish tinge to the Marquis' skin in that light. When we had finished, he sat down in the armchair and asked if I read, what I read and whether I understood what I read.

He was a friend now. He put his hand on my shoulder, looked at me with warmth in his eyes, told me not to be shy.

We would sit in our chairs reading. He taught me to think.

He told me about the development of philosophy, about poets and playwrights. We read La Mettrie's *L'Homme-machine*, a significant work, he said. According to La Mettrie nature is governed by its own laws, the universe is both organized and necessary, and good and evil are simply elements in that necessity.

'There is nothing that is intrinsically good or evil, Latour. Evil is just as necessary as good. Nature is indifferent.'

I ventured to object: 'But isn't it important for a child to learn to seek out the good and reject the bad?'

The Marquis was not attending. In a mood of sudden irritation he stood up and rammed the book back on the shelf, leaving the library without a word.

I am sure that was our last conversation about books. But a few days later he came into my room and put some volumes on my bed.

At dinner that evening he had a discussion with Madame de Montreuil. He propounded the thesis that mankind can only be defined from scientific observation and experiment. Madame spoke of the will of God. They were not listening to one another, each conducting a monologue. The Marquis was most vociferous, maintaining that man was a machine subject to desires and impulses, and that there was no point in trying to deny those impulses. Man has to follow his desires, can do nothing else, he exclaimed, scrutinizing Madame's countenance. Then he called me over and asked me to confirm La Mettrie's argument. It made me feel both proud and ashamed.

Anne-Prosphère started coming to my room at night. In her fine brocade. By the light of the moon. Her face was the colour of a gilded butterfly. I lay back on the bed, trying not to look at her, letting her chatter on. I listened to her questions about my master with my eyes closed, saying, 'I can't answer that' or 'How would I know about that?' or 'If Madame only knew you were asking such questions!'

She really did have a wonderfully shaped head. I didn't like her, but she had a beautiful head, broad across the back, a high forehead, delicate temples, a perfectly curved skull.

Outside the window, the moon. The moon had no secrets. It was supposed to inspire in us feelings of love and affection. But I knew that love was nothing more than a cloak for lust, a thirst of the mucous membranes, the age-old need to dominate another person. If people could agree to abolish the moon they would render a service to the whole of humankind.

I found my own consolation with the Swiss chambermaid, Gothon. She was too stupid to see how ugly I was. She thought I was nice, that I showed consideration and sympathy, just because I said I loved her. My master maintained that it was dangerous not to distinguish between one's own interests and those of others. 'It won't be long before you become the slave of the one you thought loved you above herself.' But Gothon's flesh was warm, and her eyes, though crooked, were pretty. She tasted of ginger and caramel. I had no desire to inflict pain on her: she did not stimulate me in that way.

I fantasized instead about the gardener's daughter. She somewhat resembled Anne-Prosphère, the same high forehead, the same curve of the cranium.

I sat down at night and made a sketch of her head.

*

Then I had an idea. I went to my master and told him that Anne-Prosphère had come to my room in the middle of the night to ask questions about him. A wonderful opportunity for seduction, I suggested. What could be more exciting than to lead an innocent girl astray? He agreed to the scheme without a moment's hesitation.

One evening, when I was walking through the park, a light in the gardener's cottage caught my eye. His daughter was leaning her head out of the window, calling to a cat in the branches of a tree just above her. I crouched down, the better to observe her, the better to stimulate my imagination. Suddenly I found myself right underneath her window, so near that I could see the arteries in her neck, smell her fragrance. I remained there with my eyes closed long after she had gone inside again. Her skin was as white as hoar frost. She was so young, and there was something vulnerable about her.

The skull bones of a child are too soft to be broken and too thin to be sawn. They have to be snipped with large scissors.

'She'll be ten this winter,' said the gardener's wife one morning when I happened to comment on a game the girl was playing. I noted in particular her mother's frisson of pride, a flushing of the temples, a faint sigh of joy, before it occurred to me that she seemed more absorbed in the roses than in her daughter's activities.

What a disgusting creature I was. That night I lay awake fantasizing. Every time I saw what I saw in my mind's eye, I felt as if I were floating upwards. The next morning I was tired and edgy.

*

I gave Anne-Prosphère a letter from the Marquis. A few sweet words about their first meeting. She coloured and hastened away. The following day she pushed a letter into my hand. She wrote like a chambermaid.

> *'Your words are most courteous, my dear brother-in-law, but can I put my trust in you? I don't know what to believe about you, though my heart is full of desire and very susceptible to sentiments such as you have expressed . . .'*

The correspondence had been set in motion.
Yet I would be the only one to reap any pleasure from it.

It was difficult for them to conceal their feelings. Anne-Prosphère's last letter was touching. Time was getting short: I overheard a conversation that morning between Madame and the Judge in which she expressed her determination to send Anne-Prosphère away to an aunt. She feared for her daughter's morals. The hour had come.

I burnt Anne-Prosphère's letters, and there was still a faint smell of ash. I sat with the Marquis' pen in my hand: how would he have replied? What was fermenting in him: lust so all-consuming that it would destroy everything it encountered? Or just bravado? I wrote a few lines about her elegant poise, her breath 'sweeter than apple blossom'. I suggested she meet him in the stables, the night before she was due to leave. I begged her to excuse my boldness, and added a couple of lines about my pounding heart, concluding 'in the hope of seeing you . . .'

I had it all worked out. After the operation I would put her in the dung cart and cover her over. The gardener had a day off the following day. I owed him a favour. I didn't think I would perform a dissection. Just dry her head, store it, and take it out on special occasions to study the shape of the skull. I was looking forward to our rendezvous.

Midnight arrived. I took my master's cloak and hat from the cupboard. I had been practising his gait. I stood half-hidden behind the horses, waiting for her. Longing for her. Soon I would hear her dainty footsteps, she would be looking anxiously in every direction, her pretty eyes wide. Then she would be running past the horses towards me, throwing herself into my arms.

I pulled my master's cloak tighter around my face.

I yearned to feel her skin, to put my lips to the skin of her neck. It must be so soft there. Does the woman one longs for smell different from all the others? Does love create an aroma of its own?

I waited.

Nothing. No dainty footsteps. No lovesick anxiety. No pent-up desire. None of the carnal joy she would feel as she pressed herself against her sister's husband and whispered to him to tickle her with the ox-whip. No blushes. No lustful sighs. Nothing. Not even exposure. She did not come. I was deeply hurt. On my master's behalf.

*

Everything I write is subject to the Great King: the brain. The organ controlling speech is hidden between the chambers of the brain. Crabs and other crustacea have no brain; the organ that controls their senses and voluntary movements is situated in the thorax. In former times the belief was that human beings thought with their hearts. But the human brain is a complex and ingenious machine, a labyrinth for which the heart would not be sufficiently capacious.

They never found the gardener's daughter. I chopped her up by the light of the moon and scattered her through the grounds. Back in my room I opened up her head and sliced the walnut into thin slivers.

I have to admit that it was difficult to identify Rouche-foucault's organs in such a young fruit. The convolutions were so small and intertwined. The lamp in my room was too weak, and it went without saying that I could only work at night. Extremely vexatious, for how could scientific investigation be pursued under such conditions?

*

Paris. It struck me again how well organised the city was. I felt ashamed: Paris reminded me of my mission, from which I had allowed my energies to be diverted. What happened in Echauffour should not have happened. I would not lose sight of my goal again. I would keep to the names on the list in the order they appeared.

I must not let myself be tempted. The power I had over these people, who did not know me and who would only see my face for a brief instant, was fragile. Power is not something we are given, it is something I create for myself, and what I have created I can just as easily destroy. I must be careful.

I would have to proceed more scientifically. Meticulously. Rationally. And patiently.

One morning I found my bed full of black hairs. I examined myself in the mirror. My hair was falling out on the left side: was I going bald? Why just on that side? I picked up the hairs, one by one, and burnt them, shook the blanket till my arms ached. I combed my fingers tenderly through my hair and it felt strangely thinner.

I read in the *Journal de Paris* that the Comte de Rochette was looking for a servant for his house in Savoy. The Count had featured regularly in the gossip columns; he was a Don Juan, a drunkard, a troublemaker. He also had one rather intriguing quality: he was said to have an inclination to experiment. He liked the dominating ladies of the brothels. The whip. He was number four on my list, a fascinating subject for my own experiments. Certain questions sprang to mind: how had he found the money to finance such a trip, to Savoy, when not so long ago he must have been so deeply in debt that he had to borrow from a moneylender in the provinces; and how could I myself get to Savoy?

The Marquis' father, the Comte de Sade, died. The Grand Seigneur. The Marquis took his father's name, and now *he* was the Comte de Sade. But he seemed tormented. He drank and drank and walked around the house full of self-reproach, muttering about the father he never knew. The house itself was falling into wrack and ruin.

I lay dozing one morning, when my master came to the door of my room. 'Would you like tea or chocolate, Monsieur?' he asked.

I sat up in bed. He was illumined by shafts of light from the window and dressed in my clothes, as a valet. For some days we had been alternating roles, as if nature had transposed us. But I did not feel superior and was ill at ease; a fear of being seen through made me angry, and I shouted at him. When I found him asleep on the chaise longue one morning I hit him with a stick, on his back and about the head. He cried like a baby, and I had to hug him.

But when the game was finally over, and I had my own clothes on again, things seemed different. Every time I saw the Marquis coming into view through a doorway I gave a start, as if seeing a travesty of myself.

Sitting in the Marquis' library, I read Descartes. The body is a machine, according to his *Treatise on Man*, Part II, 'How the Human Machine Moves'. Paragraph 16 says that the nerves in the human machine can be compared to the pipes in a fountain. They are worked by a pump and run through the whole body. There is a rational soul situated in the brain, like a water regulator, controlling the machine.

Number two on the list, the textile manufacturer, lived diagonally across from La Madeleine. I stood at the window every morning and watched him come limping out of his house, supporting himself on a silver-headed stick, and walk slowly down the garden path into his waiting carriage. His face was contorted with pain, furrowed with rage and frustration.

The organ that senses pain must be larger in those who suffer than in others. That would be a logical assumption.

So, to Monsieur Jacques. I had decided to take his brain too and I had a splendid plan, so good that it made me laugh out loud, over-loud, in fact, and I should have suppressed it: it might have been regarded as unseemly for a servant in a house such as this. I ought to have been more circumspect.

*

Monsieur Jacques had a medium-sized factory in the Faubourg St Antoine. I never saw him greet his workers. He lived alone, a man of substance but of simple habits, the proud owner of a dog. Why had he needed to borrow money from Bou-Bou? I would never have the answer to that question, and it was not important. I sat directly opposite his house against a wall, disguised as a beggar, thinking about his obvious misery and torment. He was small and thin, with hands like a child's. But it looked as if he had been the victim of an accident: his hands were covered in dark scars. Could they be burns? His eyes were large, and his enquiring expression gave him the appearance of timidity.

The night I broke into his house, through a skylight, it was raining. I was wet when I opened the door of his bedroom. I killed the dog with a deep transverse cut that severed both its carotid artery and its windpipe. Monsieur Jacques leapt out of bed, frantic. He shouted at me, limped across the room for his stick. I replied calmly that I had come to kill him and outlined the method I would use. I told him to compose himself, since there was nothing he could do about it. But he would not. He limped up and down, his voice choked with tears. He was afraid. I said it would not hurt much and that he would suffer pain no more. But he was hysterical and would not heed me. As I approached him with the scalpel he struck out at me, only succeeding in cutting himself badly. He was making far too much noise, and I saw that I would have to act quickly if he were not to thwart my plan.

I was exceptionally fast with my hands. It was not a problem for me to stab a man before he had time to defend himself. Provided I could get close enough, it was never a problem. Monsieur Jacques let me approach him because he thought he could get the better of me with those small hands of his. But they were sliced off before he knew it. I was an artist with the knife, and Monsieur Jacques was silenced.

Now he would feel no more pain.

I followed my usual *modus operandi* in the acquisition of a human brain, and then set fire to the bedroom. Climbing out through the skylight, I realized that I had put myself in great danger.

I had come to the conclusion that the best method was to use a hammer with the head filed to a broad flat point. Then if I used gentle blows there would be no shock waves to harm the fruit within. It was better of course to start from the back: there was less risk of error.

139

The dissection of cadavers is the technique for research into dead matter. I opened the parietal bone and looked down into the brain. The convolutions did not all go in the same direction, they ran crosswise, they twisted and turned, and some seemed to have no particular direction at all. Others formed pyramids, curling in spirals. Yet it seemed that this chaotic pattern was almost universal.

When I screwed up my eyes, the convolutions looked like mountain ranges in a strange and beautiful landscape.

I found the organ for memory and language. For pride, mimicry and decisiveness. For religious sentiment. But there was much still to discover. I wanted to compile a comprehensive catalogue of the parts of the human brain. I wanted to be a great anatomist.

I could not find the organ for pain.

I came to the conclusion that I would not find it until I had mapped and catalogued the whole brain.

Just three months later I killed number three on the list: Denis-Philippe Moette, natural historian and encyclopædist. He was a highly intelligent man with a fascinating brain, rather bigger than usual, more open, easier to work with. I laboured on it for hours at a time. Between the lateral and third ventricles is the thalamus. The two halves of the brain are formed like two buttocks. At the side of these I found a blood-red substance, reminiscent of a worm. Mondino de Luzzi described the function of these worms as something to do with the thought process. When a person wants to stop thinking, the 'worms' block the spirit flow between the ventricles. I removed the thalamus and made a sketch of it.

The anatomist's worst enemy is tiredness, impatience. Even Rouchefoucault used to stop when he began to get impatient. But that was exactly when I felt the need to continue, even though it was easy to do a lot of damage in half an hour, to destroy the fine symmetry. I had to take the greatest care.

I research, therefore I am. (I have started to quote!) I followed my whims and curiosity, not fearing punishment. Punishment would be a final reward. My blood irrigating the earth around the place of execution would be proof that I had been greater than myself.

*

In the summer I went on a journey with the Marquis, to Marseille, to collect a long-standing debt. We were in good humour, and the Marquis decided that we should put up at the Hôtel des Treize-Cantons, partake of a lavish meal and then stroll through the city to see the sights. At an inn by the name of La Gorge d'Or the Marquis was informed of a girl called Jeanne Nicou, and he went straight to her room. I walked back to the hotel and lay down to rest while I waited for him.

I listened to the song of the cicadas in the garden. The sound from their little bodies was exquisite, but I wished it would stop. Ephemeral things were more beautiful than anything else. I wanted to get up from my bed, open the window and shout at these six-legged loudmouths, but the noise ceased of its own accord, and I closed my eyes and let my mind wander. I toyed with the notion that some god had heard my prayer for silence, even allowing myself a little *folie de grandeur*, lying there in the dusk, picturing myself as a kind of liberator of suffering. A man who would free the world of all pain. A man of science.

At daybreak I began to make arrangements for the day's orgy. I worked my way along the quayside, searching in countless taverns and bars for young girls. I adopted an approach both over-hasty and excessively critical. I inspected pendulous breasts, long legs, inhaled many perfumes, but nothing was to my taste, everything seemed mediocre. By the time darkness fell I had only one card left in my hand, until I discovered that the lady had gone out in a boat and could not meet us until the following day, which put me in deep disfavour with the Marquis, his rebukes ringing in my ears.

The next morning found us side by side in front of the mirror, dressed exactly alike, the same wigs, the same knee-breeches and shoes, and each sporting a stick. It was the Marquis' idea that we should look as similar as possible. Part of the fore-play, was how he described it. We were on our way to an assignation with some luscious young ladies in the Rue des Capucins. We stood admiring one another in the mirror. The Marquis grinned and said, 'I think we should have nicknames. I want you to call me La Fleur.'

I looked at him in astonishment.

'And what will you call me?'

'Président.'

I was flabbergasted and just gaped at him in the mirror. Then I burst out laughing.

The Marquis chattered about everything and nothing on the way, as excited as a child as we pushed past women with baskets and traders with cartloads of fish. People stared. They stared at me, a nobleman, Monsieur le Président. The door of the house in the Rue des Capucins was open; we went in and ascended the steep staircase. I was an aristocrat.

'I am La Fleur. This is my master, Monsieur le Président.'

While the Marquis was introducing us, I inspected the girls' pale faces and high bosoms. They smiled and curtseyed and scrutinized us in their turn. But I found it difficult to understand what they said. I was an aristocrat.

Once in the room the Marquis started whipping the girls' white rumps. How he whipped them and was whipped himself!

Broad red weals across his backside. He gave the girls aniseed drops soaked in cantharides, Spanish fly, also called *pastilles de Richelieu*. These home-made sweetmeats were meant to stimulate them. I stood on the other side of the room watching the half-naked bodies, grinning at the thought of my new name and more aroused by my own clothes than by the girls' juicy orifices and reddening bottoms. Their lustful cries in response to the Marquis sounded like the squealing of animals. His face and his hands running over their hind quarters, slapping them, made me wonder at the diversity of things that arouse people. He gave them more aniseed drops. He stuck his nose between their buttocks and sniffed, in the hope that they would fart. But the girls had probably got cramp from the concoction. The Marquis was more than usually exhilarated.

'Monsieur le Président,' he cried, 'those pastilles are not effective. I'm a hopeless chemist.'

I nodded, punishing him severely with the cat-o'-nine-tails while he beat an attractive redhead with a broom. Another beautiful young girl stood over by the window holding her belly and whimpering and jabbering about her father, a Godfearing man who would apparently never hurt a soul. The girls were shrieking, and the Marquis was shrieking, and I felt as if I were being lifted up out of that madhouse and looking down from above on the bodies in the room, at open mouths and inflamed buttocks, at coins and bonbons rolling all over the floor . . .

And so passed the morning of the Spanish fly. I had to support the Marquis on the way back to the hotel: he was finding it difficult to walk.

He talked in his sleep that night, sounding troubled. I tried to make out what he was saying, but had to abandon the attempt. When I woke up, the sunlight was streaming in, and the first thing I did was to turn towards the Marquis to study his face in sleep. La Fleur, I thought, sitting up in bed and smiling to myself. I could hear children outside throwing pebbles at a fence.

The Marquis was in a hurry that morning. He wanted to leave straight away and so set me to packing. I was soon carrying the trunks downstairs to the hotel reception and assessing the cranium of the hotel owner, a mean little man with scrawny fingers and claw-like nails. The Marquis seemed nervous. He reprimanded the coachman for not having the carriage ready and then turned to the proprietor.

'If anyone asks for La Fleur and Président de Curval, we're on our way to Lyon. Got that?'

The proprietor nodded indolently, suppressing a yawn.

I put the trunks down.

Président de Curval?

My whole body froze.

'Pick up the trunks, you dolt, here comes the coach.'

I just stared at him.

'The trunks!'

I picked them up and went to the door. Out on the street he kicked me in the ribs.

'What's the matter with you?'

I stopped and stammered, 'Président de Curval?'

'Don't stand there as if you've lost your tongue, Latour. It's only a name.'

The letters danced before my eyes.

'It's just a name I used to use some time ago, that's all.'

I tried to nod.

As I heaved the trunks up on to the carriage I could still see it spelled out in front of me, letter by letter: Président de Curval. Number eight on the list.

When we were seated, I noticed that the Marquis was agitated but could not understand why. He said little and when he did speak, he sounded like a stranger. I suddenly felt I no longer knew him.

We drove through the smart streets of Aix-en-Provence, into the Lubéron towards Apt and La Coste.

I told myself I would have to forget that day, I would have to find a way of purging it from my memory. I brought all the day's events together in my mind and decided they no longer existed.

We arrived in La Coste at dusk. The château was high above the town, surrounded by olive and almond groves, but in the failing light all I could see was the steep track and the outline of the mountains behind the turrets. And I knew that even if I managed to put things out of my mind, I would still have a queasy feeling in my stomach throughout our stay.

In the mean time, one of the women from Marseille decided to make a charge against us because of the aniseed drops. When we arrived in La Coste the order for our arrest had already been signed.

The Marquis was fretful and furious and did not know what to do with himself. He reacted to the news by keeping to his chamber, while simultaneously complaining of feeling like a prisoner. He cursed the police in Marseille, ranting and roaring and venting his spleen on the judges and the whole damned legal system of France. Could a man not be free to indulge his lusts with a whore in peace? Should the law prohibit passion? At one moment he was standing on a chair and raging at the ceiling, as if it were a heaven full of vengeful gods, and the next he was lying on the floor sobbing and whining and admitting to all the guilt of the world. Renée tried to comfort him, but he could not tolerate her motherly tones and threw her out. On the other hand, our dear sister-in-law, Anne-

Prosphère, who happened to be visiting, succeeded in calming him sufficiently to get him to emerge from his chamber.

I had a brilliant idea. When the Marquis had settled down in the dining room and taken a glass of Neapolitan red wine with his asparagus soup, I went over and whispered in his ear that we might go to Savoy. The police would come to La Coste in the course of the next few days, I said. In Savoy they would not be able to touch us. The Marquis was in a state of claustrophobic panic and would have gone along with anything. He immediately declared me a genius, and his eyes sparkled.

He elected to take Anne-Prosphère with him on his flight. Silence descended on the dining room. There was rarely any guile at La Coste. The future was reflected in Madame Renée's countenance: the scandal, the newspaper articles, the shame, Anne-Prosphère's blighted marriage prospects, her mother's outrage and fury — all this was clearly visible in the pallor of her face. And when Anne-Prosphère did not reject the proposal but just stared into the Marquis' eyes with unwavering desire, Madame Renée swallowed her anger and turned her gaze inwards to a ravaged landscape where she could indulge her suffering in solitude.

I started packing again.

Shortly afterwards we were on our way from La Coste to Savoy, the mainland realm of the King of Sardinia. To immunity from the laws of France.

*

Sitting in the constricted and airless carriage, I could not stop thinking about Madame de Montreuil. Her figure appeared before me whenever I closed my eyes. I let my thoughts roam at will.

She was walking in the woods at Echauffour, raving at the

trees and weeping. 'Oh Lord, have mercy on a woman who has always honoured Your name! Inflict pox on the insane sodomite who has brought disgrace on me and bewitched my daughters, and let him soon perish. At least give him, dear Lord, a sickness that will cause his member to drop off, that flap of flesh that pertains to the most intimate act of marriage but that this cur raises aloft in all weathers and thrusts into every available orifice . . .'

Madame de Montreuil cast an apologetic glance up to the heavens.

'Forgive me, Lord, for having mentioned this at all. But You must see, in Your wisdom, that a dog such as he cannot be allowed to live?'

But the Lord did not answer her. She kicked at a tree root — and cried out in pain. Everything was conspiring against her! As she limped home she thought of all the so-called philosophers who had afflicted the country with their doubts about God and King and Church.

'How can there be a God,' she said aloud to herself, 'when he permits my son-in-law to go on living?'

She stopped, gritting her teeth: there was only one thing to be done. Divine justice would take whatever time it needed, but Madame de Montreuil could not wait that long. She would take up the scourge in her own hand. The good Marquis would not know what had hit him.

Thus I sat in the carriage giving free rein to my fantasies. But however much I might ridicule her, Madame de Montreuil was a force to be reckoned with even in the imagination.

On 11th July 1772 an officer of the Royal Courts of Justice in Apt came to La Coste with four armed men to arrest Donatien Alphonse François Comte de Sade and his valet. To the officer's surprise the valet seemed to go under four different names: Carteron, La Jeunesse, Monsieur le Président and

Latour. We were accused of sodomy and poisoning. Three prostitutes had already made statements and were under medical supervision. Two more were about to be interviewed. Madame Renée told them that her husband and his valet had left the château a week before with her sister, Anne-Prosphère. Three orders for arrest were issued and a search warrant signed, our property was confiscated, and we were summoned to present ourselves within fourteen days.

Madame de Sade went to Marseille to take up the Marquis' case and soon came to the conclusion that everyone was 'horribly prejudiced' against him. A proclamation was issued in La Coste and district demanding that we give ourselves up; then the public prosecutor intervened to set up a special tribunal to try the accused, and we were found guilty *in absentia*: the Marquis de Sade of poisoning and sodomy, I of sodomy.

The sentence ran as follows:

> *De Sade and his valet shall be taken to the cathedral in Marseille, there, attired only in prison garb, to beg forgiveness before the portal. Thereafter they shall be taken to the Place Saint-Louis, where the said Comte de Sade shall be beheaded on a scaffold, and the said Latour hanged from a gibbet until he chokes, and then the bodies of De Sade and Latour shall be burnt, and their ashes scattered to the wind.*

On 11th September the sentence was confirmed by the Parliament of Provence, and on 12th September two straw effigies representing the Marquis and myself were burnt on the Place des Prêcheurs in Aix. Now we had been executed *in absentia*.

*

What is fear? Is it a word we use when we don't know what other words to use?

I was afraid. Yet I longed for danger, pain, my own destruction.

We never talked about the verdict, nor the execution of the straw effigies, but I sometimes thought all this had made the Marquis weaker and full of self-loathing.

Would I have felt pain at the instant of death?

I was aware of her smell. She sat in the swaying carriage reading Rousseau's *Confessions* with a smile on her lips. She had delicate lines on her neck and smelt of something I had forgotten, something I could not manage to put into words, but which was as sharply and clearly defined as the aroma of peppermint. She had reconciled herself to everything and was concealing her nervousness: she would love her sister's husband and pretend to be his wife. It was shameful that I was so obsessed with her. It was a betrayal of my master.

We crossed into Savoy and continued to Florence. There we admired Titian's *Venus*, and a friend of the family, Doctor Mesny, showed us his rare collection of specimens: fossils, antique coins — and a wax model of a young woman. The model could be opened and used for the teaching of anatomy. The Marquis had numerous questions about the 'young woman's' internal organs, to which the doctor responded, while I stood observing the Marquis' inquisitive face.

We journeyed on to Rome. My master was introducing himself now as the Comte de Mezan and Anne-Prosphère as his wife. I was Carteron, d'Armand and Señor Quiros.

Anne-Prosphère said to me one day, 'We'll move to Savoy, Latour, and settle there. I am his wife now. We love each other. We need you.'

That was a flattering exaggeration. From the tone of her voice I could tell they were in fact bored with one another. Only lust remained, and she was in despair.

Savoy was part of the western Alps, belonging to the King of Sardinia, bordering Italy in the east and the *départements* of Isère and Ain in the west. We rode along roads carved out of the hillside until we arrived in the capital, Chambéry. I had never experienced such clear air, and at night, as I was about to drift into dreams, I felt I should not let myself fall asleep completely, lest the thin air cause harm to my brain by depriving it of oxygen.

We rented a house from a nobleman, just outside the city walls. I bought furniture and drapery and bedclothes from a merchant by the name of Ansard, who told me where the Comte de Rochette lived, how many servants he had and who his circle of friends were. I discovered that he was the youngest son of a very rich family, but that according to rumour he had squandered the best part of his inheritance.

*

The Marquis and Anne-Prosphère had withdrawn. Desire had driven them into one another and entangled them so firmly that they had gone silent. The silence was difficult to cope with. They never left the house. They saw nobody, except for the servants and a loquacious naturalist lodging at a hotel in the town. They ordered their food from a nearby restaurant and ate without talking to each other. They lived as the Comte de Mezan and his wife, and so discreetly that I began to think they no longer existed. At night they made love: the sounds of the pain of lust.

Then the faint notes of discord reached my ears: the time of silence had come to an end.

A few weeks later Anne-Prosphère quitted the house, and the Marquis locked himself in his room. I went to a brothel to weep away my sorrows in a woman's embrace.

That night I paid a visit to the house of the Comte de Rochette. Number four. I stood for several hours watching the darkened building. In the morning the servants appeared first, and I continued my vigil until I caught sight of the Count. A tall, spindly man. He came out on to the square to receive a lawyer from Chambéry, looking at him with the deferential, rather ingratiating smile of a man who has waited too long for something he regards as his right. Although tall, the Count moved like a much smaller man. By the time he had gone indoors again I had decided what I would do with him. So I went home.

But I soon returned and spent an entire week becoming conversant with his various occupations. He was a keen amateur botanist. He would ride out in search of rare flowers in the mountains or take lengthy walks alone in the valley meadows.

The Marquis directed at me the whole of his frustration at Anne-Prosphère's departure. He berated me for the least little thing, corrected me, gave me impossible tasks and then punished me when I didn't accomplish them to his satisfaction. I sensed he was keeping me under observation and that he suspected I had plans he knew nothing of.

The Count's day of judgement was nigh.

I trailed him on foot one morning as he rode out. He ambled along at a leisurely pace, continually stopping to squint up at the sun.

His cerebellum was hard, whereas his cerebrum was very soft. Rouchefoucault postulated that the animal instincts were centred in the cerebellum, beneath the cerebral hemispheres. The organ for the sense of pain must be nearby. I worked with infinite precision, locating the nerves, holding the muscle fibres to one side with tweezers, removing flesh and fat and tracing the nerves down into the depths with my scalpel, taking the utmost care not to damage the muscles.

The nerves are the servants and messengers of the brain. They are not easy to see, but without them the brain would not function as a machine.

I was dissecting out in the meadows. I found a nerve that I was convinced must lead to the centre of pain. Cutting slowly and exactly with my scalpel, I watched the nerve emerging from the surrounding tissue and managed to follow it, to isolate it. Several times I nearly lost it, but it did not escape me. Now I must be close to the centre.

Twilight was approaching, but I chose to ignore it. In an hour's time it would be so dark that I would start making mistakes. Yet I could not hurry. I had to work carefully. My hand was seizing up with cramp.

The nerve is a pathway. I had to follow it patiently, and my heart was hammering in my breast.

Then clouds covered the sun, and the scalpel slipped into the tissue around the nerve and severed the muscles and veins.

I lay back on the soggy turf with the damp penetrating my shirt. Looking up at the lowering skies, I could see that it would soon start to rain. And even as I lay there I felt the first splashes on my face.

Exhausted, I made my way through the woods towards my master's house.

I didn't think anyone would identify the remains I left behind me. A hunter or another botanist finding the four stakes in the stream might wonder what had gone on there but would probably attribute them to some kind of trap for large animals. Only if he set about digging up the marshy soil would he discover any human remains. And he would find the ashes of the Count's clothes. He might possibly suspect the agony suffered at that spot. Perhaps, or perhaps not. As far as I was concerned there was no more to say. The day of judgement was over. But ultimately I had failed.

The Marquis' behaviour was becoming distinctly odd. He would go for long rides and stay away from the house for much of the time. Discretion, which he had made a virtue of by necessity, was no more. He had stopped carping and criticizing, but he would stare, stare, stare, with a look I had never seen in him before. At night he sat writing. He was avoiding me. Had he developed an *idée fixe* that I was responsible for Anne-Prosphère's departure?

One morning I found him drenched with sweat in his bed. He was in great pain, and it did not take me long to ascertain that he had an abscess on his stomach. I rode over to the Hôtel Pomme d'Or and found that there was an excellent surgeon in the locality, Monsieur Thonin, whom I persuaded to drop everything and come to the house immediately. He bled the Marquis.

I nursed him for ten days. He rambled incoherently but said things that struck fear into me, things he ought not to have known. He made remarks about me that caused me to wonder even more whether he had been spying on me, whether he had been keeping me under surveillance.

I went down with a fever myself. I sat by the Marquis' bed, sweating and dozing. We both had delirious fantasies. Then as he improved, the fever seemed also to dry out of my own body.

I saw the horses galloping out of the wood as I was standing in the kitchen, already facing that direction as if I were expecting them. The smell of boiled tongue and sugared almonds wafted around me, and the cook was complaining that we had no bread and no pepper or nutmeg for the sauce, but her voice seemed far away. The three riders came right up to the house. The Major, in shiny boots, dismounted and strode quickly to the door. I ran up to the Marquis' room to warn him. But he waved me away: he could flee no more.

Major de Chevanne and his two adjutants kept a close watch on us as the Major declared the Comte de Mezan under arrest. At the instance of Madame de Montreuil, the king's foreign minister, the Duc d'Aiguillon, had asked the Sardinian Ambassador in Paris to have him arrested and imprisoned for an indefinite period. The Marquis muttered a few curses, his face twisted, resigned. His body was taut, invulnerable, a bastion against the world.

The next morning we were driven to the castle of Miolans.

'I haven't committed any crime. Why are you arresting me?' the Marquis exclaimed angrily to the adjutants. 'Don't I even get a trial? What kind of state is it that arrests innocent citizens without even hearing their explanations? What other unspeakable acts has the Sardinian government on its conscience?'

But they sounded like well-rehearsed phrases, and to me all he said was, 'This is the worst thing that could happen.'

The castle of Miolans was some distance from Chambéry, on a vertiginous outcrop, three hundred metres above the valley of the Isère. Three walls and two moats encircled the prison. The Marquis' cell was in the castle keep in the middle of the central courtyard, the keep serving as both a prison and the commandant's quarters. The cell faced south and had a view of the valley and the snow-clad Alps.

A dark stone floor, intersected by a strip of light from the window. Dark stone walls. An open fireplace. That was one of our privileges, the Sardinian government's recognition of the Marquis' status as an aristocrat. And a few days later came the ultimate pat on the back: I would be allowed to serve my master in prison, to come and go, under guard, so that I could purchase provisions for him.

I deserved the punishment, of course, and should have been allowed to expiate my guilt instead of my master. But that was not how it was: I was there for his so-called crimes, not my own. It was clear to me now that a crime does not exist until it is discovered by the law.

My cadavers, I called them, the bodies that had been my assistants in my scientific research. Was there an unwritten law implanted in everyone? If there were such a thing I must certainly have violated it. But what was the appropriate sentence for having broken an unwritten law?

My dissection of the Count continued to haunt me; it had been scientifically so badly conducted. I was critical of my own technique and intent on improving it. But there was something else worrying me too, though I was not sure what it was. Something about the situation that I could not get out of my mind: the valley, the Count, the horse, the twilight. Whenever I thought about it I had an uncomfortable tingling sensation on the nape of my neck.

My master was ranting and raving still, exploding at the slightest little thing. He complained repeatedly about De Launay, the commandant, writing long letters of protest to the Sardinian government and ridiculing the prison warders for their 'supreme stupidity'. I tried to cheer him up with stories of escapes, but it was impossible to improve his mood.

All the way along the route of his exercise walks round the keep, past the curtain walls and the underground cell from which the moaning of a crazed prisoner could be heard, down the path to the kitchen garden and on past the chapel in the lower tower, across the courtyard and back to the cell, all through this daily exercise the Marquis would curse 'the criminal imbeciles who are keeping me locked up'.

He would spit and cough in bitter resentment. 'They're more contemptible than the fish merchants of Aix foisting off their rotten tuna. They're the lackeys of torturers. Madame de Montreuil's bile is spewed over me even down here, Latour, letters of such unfathomable inanity and malice that you would think I had never cared for Renée and my children, never been a devoted son who loved his parents. Am I a monster just because I have amused myself with a few women of the street? Do I not deserve to live?'

I put my hand on his arm — in prison we were of equal worth, or equal worthlessness — and said, 'You are the best man France has.'

Twice a week I went down to Chambéry to fetch the Marquis whatever he might desire: eau de Cologne, orange-blossom water, vanilla bonbons, paper and ink, brandy, candles, medicaments. I did not enjoy these trips out into freedom. I spoke to people as little as possible, tried not to see them as bodies. I wanted to be back inside the castle; I liked the prison life.

No matter how much I brought him, my master was still dissatisfied. Looking at him for signs of optimism, I saw nothing. His whining continued. He suffered headaches, chest pains and an abscess and constantly had to have new medicines.

He talked incessantly, over-stimulating himself, bursting with explanations, anecdotes, ideas. He spoke of God's evil, of nature's 'malevolent molecules' and of his own immorality as if it had been inherent in him since birth. He tried to excuse himself with rational arguments — for a crime he had not committed. I feared he was living in the shadow of his reputation.

I lay dreaming of a world of stone, of what awaited me in

Paris: the bodies of numbers five, six and seven. Body number eight was lying breathing beside me here. But I tried not to think about that.

His face was contorted in pain. Was pain a piece of theatre, or was it real? The Marquis had always made a game of pain. At night we would talk about brothels and young female bodies. He spoke of the cruelty of women and maintained that society would be a better place if women whipped their husbands more often. It would spare us from women spreading their venom in other ways. He talked about pain, this resentful nobleman lay on a prison bed fantasizing about tyranny, about the pleasure he found in the physical suffering of others. His constant burbling made me feel ill.

I would fall asleep to the sound of his voice.

I would lie dreaming in a world of stone.

One morning I awoke to hear his groaning. I turned in my bed and found his broad face right up against mine. He was suffering; I could see his grimaces even in the dark, like a language of his own, a language only I understood.

Another morning an Italian made an attempt to escape. He got half way over the second wall before the guards caught him. The prisoners stood at their windows and heard him screaming as he was dragged off. After that there was silence in Miolans.

A few weeks later we were making plans with the Baron de l'Allée, a notorious swindler and former escaper.

The Marquis had asked the commandant if he could take his meals in the lower tower nearer the kitchen, since the food was often cold by the time it reached his table, and the Marquis made it clear that he found it totally unacceptable to have to eat cold food. The commandant had orders to allow him certain privileges and so granted his request. Next to the room in which we were now to eat was the cook's storeroom. Baron de l'Allée had been in to investigate and discovered that it had a window without a grille, the only one in the whole fortress. He thought it was big enough to climb through. Five metres below lay freedom.

The room was kept locked, but the cook had a key.

I went to the kitchen to fetch the midday meal for the Baron and the Marquis. As I poured the soup into bowls and put the chicken on their plates, arranged the marinated artichokes and filled the wine carafe, I thought again of Paris and what awaited me there, numbers five, six and seven. And number eight. But it made me feel dizzy to think too much.

The cook, a short, fat man, had just gone to the dining room, and I knew he would be back in the kitchen in two minutes. He would kick open the door and come rushing in. So I took up position by the door, holding my tray at arms' length, and listened for the sound of his footsteps. Along he came, humming a tune, kicked the door open, and chicken and artichokes flew across the floor, the wine soaked my jacket, the cook cursed and shouted and got down on the floor to pick up the food and put it back on the plates, while I apologized profusely, bent over him and managed to extract the key from his pocket. He spun round and lashed out at me.

'What the hell do you think you're doing?'

I winked at him, whereupon he pushed me away without noticing that his keys were missing. I went back to the Marquis' cell, lit a candle and put a letter from the Marquis on the table. It warned the commandant against trying to recapture us: his private army, the Marquis had written, was waiting for us. Then I returned to the lower tower, served the meal, and we stuffed ourselves with chicken, gulped down the soup and wine and unlocked the door to the storeroom. With the aid of a rope provided by the Baron we let ourselves down into the moat, swam to the other side and sped off through the forest towards the French border.

We ran for several hours and when we reached the border we ran on for yet another hour before we stopped. The Marquis and the Baron lay concealed in the bushes and slept while I kept watch. Through the foliage I could see the Marquis' head and I could hear the Baron snoring. I was trembling with cold and fatigue and kept my feet tucked under me. My face was caked in dried sweat. I sat staring at the Marquis' head. Every time I tried to get up and go over to him I felt sick. It was quite incomprehensible. I sat there the whole night without moving. When dawn broke I came to the conclusion that it was foreordained: I would never be able to bring myself to kill the Marquis.

*

Paris — in the spring. The new light was reflected in the Seine and up on to the banks, illuminating the trees from within, transforming the leaves into gleaming gold. I walked about the city, enjoying its smells and the sight of the people. But after a while the bright sunlight began to irk me, giving me the uncomfortable sensation that someone was staring at me, as if the sun were a great eye.

My anatomical instruments had been abandoned in Savoy, so I'd had to acquire new ones, which I was now carrying in my coat pocket.

Number five on my list was the Benedictine monk, Father Noircuill.

I stood staring down into the chaos of the gyri for an hour, contemplating the mysterious interweavings. There lay the monk's faculties and characteristics, logic and confusion. Pain must be somewhere between the nerve fibres and the blood vessels.

I didn't believe that evil stemmed from the brain but in the aqueduct of Sylvius, in the fissure or space dividing the two hemispheres.

But I no longer had the same degree of patience.

Something had happened.

I couldn't understand it. Ever since returning from Savoy I had been afflicted by a feeling of nausea and discomfort. It was not pain. Just discomfort and nausea. What could it be? Could someone have infected me? I could not understand it.

*

I was back in La Coste. It was the harshest winter for many years, with thick rime on the fields. The windows were iced up, the countryside completely silent. I myself was very uneasy. I had never felt so uneasy. Something was bothering me, but I had no idea what it was. I did no work, no dissection, made no notes, read nothing, did nothing.

That winter I saw many remarkable things and experienced remarkable pleasures. Nanon the procuress, the braids of her red hair tied to the ceiling. Du Plan, a dancer from the Comédie de Marseille, who had adorned his room with the bones of a dead baron. Rosette from Montpellier who craved the cat-o'-nine-tails and the thrilling numbness after the pain. Gothon's naked buttocks over the edge of the table. My palms burning. The new gleam in Renée's eyes. The five young girls, her 'seamstresses', who were laid shrieking over the sewing table. And the Marquis himself. I was witness to an apparently endless and desperate orgy. Was it pleasure or consolation? It was as if the months in Fort Miolans had knocked the joy out of us. I found it impossible to sleep at night; I thought too much, asked too many questions. Why were we doing this? Why were we so aroused by all these bizarre activities? What was I doing here? I had the feeling that everything was falling apart, that I was going nowhere, with no direction. Had I lost all sense of purpose?

I was not working, perhaps that was it. Perhaps that was the cause of my unease.

An unaccountable impulse made me get dressed and go for a walk across the frosty fields. By derelict barns, in the corners of fields stood Belial, Morax and Focalor . . . shadowy figures with weirdly coloured eyes . . . decrepit but somehow cheerful demons with faces in which nothing was in quite the right place . . . They were making a fire by the light of the moon and talking about the end of time . . . I had no memory of how I got back to the château. I lay on my bed, staring at the ceiling, sweating and wondering whether I had seen visions.

Suddenly it was all over, the fucking, the flagellation, the gorging, corruption, fury, ecstasy. The end came in the form of an emissary from Paris. My master's mother was dying. The Marquis sat motionless with the letter in his hand. Then he whispered to me, without raising his eyes from the letter, told me to send all the servants home, all the maids, everyone except Gothon and myself. He would go to Paris immediately.

Once again I was sitting in the carriage with my master. We left the inn before daybreak, the other carriage containing Renée and Gothon following on behind. It was as dark inside as outside. You could just make out the shape of the mountains above, an azure blue rim on the horizon. The carriage sped over stones and mud, through overhanging branches, the wooden seats digging into my thighs. The Marquis was asleep, or so I thought. But then there was a sound as of a throat being cleared, and I could see the light in his eyes as his voice came out of the darkness, and he began to speak of the mother he hardly knew and about the Condé Palace.

'There were a thousand doors in the palace. I would run along the corridors and shout in at every open door, in case there was somebody there. I was a boisterous child, and my mother's hands were too delicate to control me. I was spoilt, a little despot. I always got my own way, even changed my mind and had my way again. Then Prince Louis-Joseph de Bourbon arrived, my cousin for whom my mother had responsibility. He was four years older than me, and they wanted me to call him brother, but I refused. He was still mourning the death of his parents. Oh, and how he was comforted! He pretended to be ill. He was the son of Monsieur le Duc, with blood bluer than ours, and thought he owned the whole world. I saw him in my mother's bedroom, snuggling up against her belly. It made me spew, and I was sick for three days afterwards. We used to play in the courtyard between the two wings of the house, among the flowerbeds. Or we would play at cards in the library. He would alter the rules and he was better at cheating than I was. But I was wild and would fly at him, and he used to run under the stairs in tears. My mother cried when she saw his bloody face. She said he looked as if he had been beaten by a grown man. But she didn't punish me. I wanted her to punish me, to hit me hard, but she didn't. She sent me away, first to an aunt in Avignon, then to the abbot's castle, and so it went on. When I was ten I came back to Paris to study with the Jesuits. By that time I no longer recognized my mother.'

The Marquis closed his eyes, and for a moment I thought he had not wanted to confide in me. But then I heard him panting as if he were trying not to weep.

Well, she would soon be dead anyway. As dead as Bou-Bou.

So what? He scarcely knew her. What was he losing? Nothing. Only what he had never had. What would he miss? Only something he had never had. Could there be such a thing? Was that love, or hatred? And what did he have left? Nothing. Oblivion. Wine. Whores. So what did he have left? A prick, a whip, a pair of eyes. And an evil dream that could never be realized, a dream that would wipe out all humanity and the sun.

The carriage rolled up in front of the Hôtel de Danemark in the Rue Jacob. There was a message in reception for the Marquis: his mother was already dead. The funeral would take place in a few days' time. He received the news with his eyes averted. I went with him to his room. He said nothing. Once inside, he lay on the bed, his breathing still heavy, and sank into the bedclothes like a formless lump of meat.

'I wouldn't have recognized her anyway,' he mumbled, then fell silent as if he would never utter a single word again. I went over to the bed and, angered by his exhausted face, bowed deeply and asked if it would not be a good idea to go to a brothel and indulge ourselves, to put him in a better humour perhaps. He looked up at me dully, remained silent and closed his eyes.

I bent over him, but as I was reaching for the scalpel in my pocket I felt a sudden surge of nausea and had to turn away.

I locked the door of the room as I left. A lame servant passed me in the corridor. I went to the head of the stairs and leaned against the banister rail, feeling weak, the taste of bile in my mouth, trying to breathe more calmly myself.

In the reception hall below stood Inspector Marais in high boots and gold buttons, scanning the area with his experienced eyes. He must have been informed of the Marquis' arrival. I stood for a moment looking at this figure of authority. Could this be the end? A sudden panic.

I backed away from the stairs, removed my shoes and ran

barefoot along the corridor. I clambered out on to the roof through a half-open window, slipped on the wet tiles but managed to grab on to a skylight. Bending my knees, I peered over my shoulder to the street below. It was a long way down. I could hear voices from below. One of Marais' officers stepped out of a carriage. All my weight was on the skylight, but it held firm. There was Inspector Marais leading a prisoner, Marais and the Marquis, walking slowly across the street, an officer opening the door of the carriage, me hanging on to the skylight, it holding firm, Marais pushing the Marquis into the carriage and climbing in after him, me hanging on to the skylight, it holding firm, the carriage trundling off, me banging my fist on the skylight and sliding down the tiles, the carriage trundling along the street, me sliding down the steep roof, trying to turn, seeing the street below, like a cavernous mouth, the carriage disappearing, trying to get a grip on loose tiles but cutting myself, tumbling sideways, falling outwards into emptiness.

5

Inspector Ramon

Father Noircuill, the Benedictine monk, was unrecogniz-
able.

'And he used to have such a gentle face,' someone whispered
in the background, the voice merging with the sound of the
river. All Inspector Ramon could hear was his own internal
voice repeating the refrain, 'Who was he? How did he get
here?' He dropped to his knees to take a better look at the
now headless monk. The body had been washed up on the left
bank of the Seine in the early hours of the morning and found
by a beggar who had been sleeping against one of the boats
drawn up on the bank. That too angered the Inspector, because
the Prefect of the Paris region and the city police had issued
orders that all beggars throughout the country should be
arrested. Their place was in prison, not on the streets. Even
though Ramon thought it absurd to waste police time round-
ing up the homeless he had immediately put the man in handcuffs, because Ramon was a dutiful policeman. Ten years in
the army had taught him that obedience was the most
comfortable way of life. Having been promoted to detective
inspector in the Sûreté, he found himself in an unaccustomed
situation: his was now the mouth giving orders, his the finger
pointing the direction, his the role of infallible logician. In the
first few months he had felt panic-stricken. He had heard his

own words like a remote echo and questioned his own statements as if he were still a subordinate, with the veiled criticism of a subordinate. He saw himself reflected in his men's eyes and was well aware of the mockery behind their deferential expressions. He knew the destructive power of subterfuge. Gradually he had discovered that the best method of self-protection was to follow the rules in every particular. Meticulousness and sense of duty.

He stood up and gave the stocky corpse a shove with his boot, so that it rolled over on to its side, and then crouched down again to study it closer. There were scratches on the shoulder, and the hood was ripped to shreds. The monk had evidently put up quite a fight. Ramon drew a cross with his finger by the monk's shoulder in the sand and then examined the amputation itself, a neat and tidy job attesting to a thorough knowledge of bones and sinews. The murderer must have had some experience of dissection. Ramon had ordered his men to search for the head, but after four hours they had not found so much as a hair. He told them to carry on looking, ignoring the reluctance in their expressions. He scrutinized again the cut that had severed the head from the body: it was remarkably even.

There was a shout from one of his men and Ramon straightened up and looked towards the three young officers standing in a group with their backs towards him. He went over to them half-heartedly, certain that it would be some ridiculous triviality to distract his concentration to no purpose, and brusquely asked what it was.

'This, sir, I've found this.'

The officer was holding up a half-moon-shaped fragment of tooth.

Checking the monk's hands, he found a cut on his left knuckle. The peaceable monk had lunged out at his assailant and struck him a well-directed blow.

Back at the police station Ramon wrote a report for his superiors, in which he stated that the monk had been killed with a scalpel and the head severed from the body and not found at the scene. He gave a general description of the victim and ended with a note: 'See cases 1-5, in file labelled "The Anatomist".' There was no doubt in his own mind that this murder was linked to those five other mysterious deaths in Paris in the last few years. The murderer's technique was too individual to be imitated. In a postcript he added, 'It is to be hoped that the Edict of 1656, Article 9 of which banned begging in the city, might aid the apprehension of this most vile of criminals. Officers should be detailed to question all beggars in custody.' Ramon was pleased with that little addition. He was sure the Prefect would appreciate his familiarity with the relevant laws.

In his own home later that evening he was in pensive mood. Nothing was insoluble; there was always a solution to everything. After his elderly mother had bade him good night, and he had carried her to bed as she requested and opened the window, and she had made her usual remark on that, asking him to open it a little more, and he had done so and pulled up the bedcovers and bent over her face that smelt of sour cheese to kiss her hairy cheek, after he had done all that, as he did every single evening in exactly the same way, he went out again, something he normally never did. No, when he thought about it, it was a year since he had last left the house after dark. He walked the length of several streets, feeling the fresh air doing him good.

When he returned, he settled himself in the best chair and thought, 'Now, let's go over the cases I've had in recent years and think clearly about each one of them, without drawing any hasty conclusions — if I do that, if I just think straight, sooner or later I'll come across something I've overlooked: a hidden motive.'

He sat there for about an hour, letting his thoughts range more or less as intended, but without result. Finally he said to himself, 'If I sit down for an hour every evening and use my reason, if I concentrate my thoughts properly, I'm bound to solve this case in the end.'

Satisfied with his resolution, he went into the bedroom and performed an ingenious ritual. It consisted principally of moving everything in the room into new positions, forming one of seven different arrangements. The intention of the procedure, which had to be exact to have any validity, was to create a distinct order for every day of the week. He liked waking up in the morning and being able to look round the room and know that it was a completely new day, and that nothing, not even the position of the simplest ornaments in his room, was the same as the day before.

It had started seven years earlier, and he had followed the same routine in every particular ever since. He had felt a compulsion to do it at a time he still thought of as 'an incomprehensible year'. Seven years ago he had suddenly developed an overwhelming feeling of meaninglessness. He had been investigating suspect writers, under the supervision of Inspector d'Hémery, to check whether their works contained any elements of blasphemous or politically undesirable material. In various disguises he had visited cafés frequented by writers and artists and listened to the pretentious chatter of publishers and literary men. He had read thousands of books and pamphlets in the course of the same period, but only a handful of cases had led to convictions. Then one morning he opened a book and read a story that made such an impression on him that he considered leaving the police force altogether. It was a description of deeds ascribed to the old king of Achem, in the Kingdom of Malaya. It was a straightforward and indignant text, of little interest to the police, but the acts of tyranny depicted so luridly began to haunt Ramon every night as he tried to get to sleep. As soon as he put his head on the pillow and closed his eyes, instead of falling asleep he was sucked down into a maelstrom of horrors. It had become increasingly unintelligible to him, a pointless experience from which he could learn nothing. The events portrayed in the book did not really concern him at all, and neither the book nor the author were accorded any further attention by the police. Every single image in his nightmares emanated from that book, there was nothing of himself in them: an unknown writer's description of unknown characters in an unknown country went on obstinately whirling round in his dreams, behaving as if they were campaigning for a just cause. They reminded him of the odd feeling he had had after his father's death many years before, that there was a demon inside him thinking negative thoughts, wanting to destroy all the good he believed in.

Now he had the same sensations again. Then he had been exhausted after many weeks with little sleep, he had had a bad back and some difficulty in walking and had developed a staccato mode of speech and a hatred of anything to do with books and writers. But it was only when he woke up one morning and knew he was going mad that he became rational and told himself there was a solution to everything. The fact that he was unable to make his way from the bed to the door without knocking several things over would help him find a solution.

He had been through the files of all the murders in Paris for the last five years, had suffered eyestrain from the constant re-reading but had failed to discover any motive in the unsolved cases. There were no witnesses to the murders, and none of the regular police informers knew anything. He could see no pattern to the crimes. The victims were neither robbed nor raped, nor could he find any suggestion of revenge. In each case the assailant had removed the heads, and they were never found. Ramon felt ashamed every time he stood over a headless corpse: it was as if the murderer were giving him a message, 'I am invisible'. Did it enhance his pleasure to think he was tantalising those who were pursuing him? Ramon asked himself the same question again and again: what was the murderer's intention?

For Ramon, who saw himself as a rational and practical person, it was more than annoying. It disturbed his sleep. On his days off he found some consolation in reading political commentaries in newspapers and pamphlets and listening to young men talking about a more just and egalitarian France. The arguments for change were coherent, the language was sober, tones dispassionate. Not long ago he had listened to a young lawyer in the Châtelet and been struck by his firmly held views and sense of justice. His appreciative audience, on the other hand, had found it hard to restrain themselves, and Ramon himself had been momentarily swept along on a tide of emotion. Ramon had nothing against change, as long as it took place on the basis of rational analysis. He understood the demands for the rights of the third estate, and he sympathized with those calling for a new constitutional order. He felt anger on behalf of people of his own lowly background when he read about the way some had to slave for the nobility and the priesthood. Knowing that the landed gentry were extracting every last *sou* from poverty-stricken families who could only just survive on chestnut gruel, seeing the heaps of new-born infants lying on the church steps every morning in filthy rags in the hopes that someone would baptize them — that enraged him. But he had the good sense to keep his mouth shut about his sympathies and to do what was expected of him. He had enough worry as it was with his own cases.

He made his assistants comb through the records again, he put pressure on informers in the underworld and called in earlier witnesses for fresh interrogation. 'Even animals have a reason for killing,' he thought. 'If I can find the reason, I can find the man. There's a solution to everything.'

A few days later, as he stood chatting to a bookseller on the Pont Neuf, his eyes lit upon a medical pamphlet in one of the boxes. The cover was illustrated with the drawing of a skull, annotated with the numbers 1-19. He picked it up.

Hoffmann and Rouchefoucault
Cranial Theory

He perused it with interest. Diagrams of skulls, marking of points, lists of faculties, explanations. He turned inquiringly to the bookseller, holding the pamphlet up to view.

'It's the latest scientific fad,' the man replied good-naturedly. 'Nowadays everything has to be experimented on. They even want to mess about with our heads. These intellectual types think they can tell everything about you just by looking at your skull.'

Ramon went straight home to read the booklet. It explained Rouchefoucault's theories in spirited language. 'The great anatomist's conclusions are based on hundreds of dissections. His cranial theory is the result of unique skills and brilliant analytical insight. Rouchefoucault has solved the riddle of the human brain.' In the posterior portion of the brain lay instincts and inclinations, Ramon read, while the finer feelings were directly beneath the crown. The organs of knowledge were in the frontal lobe. The more Ramon read of the anatomist and his theories, the more convinced he became that these were important discoveries, a milestone for science. It was all so self-evident: of course there was an organ for every human faculty, such as reason and jealousy, in the same way that the lungs and heart had their distinctive functions. It was entirely logical. Ramon was impressed by the enthusiasm that underlay the presentation.

But when he had finished reading and leaned back in his chair he began to feel more ill at ease. Could the murderer be a doctor, an anatomist, driven by obsession, hunting for corpses? Scientific insanity, the complete opposite of what he had just been reading? He felt unsure of what to do. Should he start searching for his murderer in anatomy theatres? His gut feeling told him that was the right course. But his brain told him an investigation among anatomists and professors would hardly be very popular with his superiors. He decided to wait for a while.

*

Latour still woke up in the middle of the night with the sensation of being in free fall, and he could actually feel the street sucking him down from below, the air pushing against his face, his eyes watering, the street receiving him.

His body had been a broken shell for many months. He had managed to drag himself off the street, get to an inn and into a bed. He had spent the whole summer there, dreaming of pain, watching his wrecked body in some miraculous way heal itself.

It was extraordinary. But the sense of being in free fall did not disappear. He did not feel close to the ground; everything seemed a long way away. At first it was a pleasant feeling, as if his body were longing to fall and still be whole. But then he began to experience the urge to fall as a dark desire, almost a death-wish.

He thought no more about the Marquis. But something was missing from his life. He was uncertain whether it was his fall from the roof or losing the Marquis that had disorientated him, thrown him off balance and made everything familiar seem strange.

*

'Number six.'

Latour stood looking at the old seamstress. She was sitting on a little stool by the door of the workroom. All her sewing things and piles of material lay on the floor around her. He had felt in a good mood ever since he had left the inn where he was staying. He'd had a feeling he would be lucky today, would find her today. Number six. But as he approached the workroom he had become increasingly agitated and had to stop on the corner of the street to take deep breaths and try to still the uncomfortable prickling in his chest and stomach. It was again as if someone were staring at him, as if he could not escape the watchful gaze of someone unknown. He'd had the same feeling immediately before the murder of the monk. In the end he managed to continue, but the elated mood in which he had awoken had disappeared. He pulled his hat down over his eyes and went over to her. He crouched on his haunches and tried to make his voice sound reassuring.

'Madame . . . Madame. I'm looking for Madame Arnault.'

The old woman stared at him with colourless eyes but made no response. He leaned closer, and his voice became tense.

'Madame Arnault!'

She heard him that time.

'Madame Arnault . . . Madame Arnault . . .'

Her pinched shrivelled lips were trembling.

'That's right, Monsieur, that's right. Madame Arnault . . .'

She blinked in satisfaction.

175

'What's right, Madame?'

'Madame Arnault. She's got a blind daughter, hasn't she? That's right. Isn't it, Monsieur?'

Latour glanced down at the pieces of cloth on the floor in front of her; they seemed to be cut for one-legged trousers, and he could not understand how they could be sewn together to make a usable garment.

'What is it you're making, Madame?'

She seemed taken aback.

'Trousers, Monsieur, knee-breeches. Just ordinary knee-breeches, like the ones you're wearing yourself.'

Latour pulled out a coin.

'Let me order a pair from you. I really need a new pair.'

The woman grinned.

'Can you tell me where this Madame Arnault lives?'

The woman nodded, as the coin dropped into her gnarled hand.

'As far as I know she lives in a room next to a pension in the Faubourg St Antoine called the Maison Elite. What size, Monsieur? What size are the breeches?'

With what money he had left Latour ate a simple dinner at a nearby restaurant and, as night descended on the city, he set off for the Faubourg St Antoine. The thought of Madame Arnault having a blind daughter excited him at first. The most exquisite and arousing way of doing it would be to kill Madame Arnault while the daughter was in the room but without her understanding what was going on. It would enhance his pleasure if he could watch the blind girl and sense her fear while he silently worked on the old woman. But then the same feeling of anxiety descended on him again, the feeling of being observed.

Someone was watching him, judging him, keeping an eye on him. He forced himself to keep walking and not to turn round. He knew he would endanger his whole plan if he appeared nervous. He still had three people left on the list before he could rest content. If he were to be apprehended now, it would all have been in vain.

He thought about the dissection he would be performing that night into the early hours of the morning. He went over it in detail, deciding on the instruments he would use and the incisions he would make. That restored his equanimity somewhat.

He climbed into Madame Arnault's room through a skylight. He had walked straight into the Maison Elite, a dismal hostelry, sneaked past the receptionist and got out on to the roof through an open balcony door. He lay still on the roof for several hours, muttering to himself, fantasizing. When he finally opened the skylight and lowered himself into the room he felt as if he were being lifted up in the air. He trod barefoot across the cold floor, groped his way to where the blind girl lay sleeping, and stood looking at her for a few minutes before going over to the mother and killing her without eliciting so much as a groan from her aged throat.

*

Ramon was in his office, full of indignation, as he often was when alone. The streets of Paris were ringing with gossip about the police being on the trail of the murderer by now popularly known as the 'Anatomist'. But the talk was much exaggerated. Wild rumours and idle speculation infuriated Ramon. He had just that morning heard new reports from the underworld. The murderer, according to criminal sources, was a person connected with the Palace, one of the king's vassals, whom the police would be unlikely to arrest. Ramon leapt up from his chair and went to the window. 'Steady on,' he admonished himself, stretching his neck to relax the muscles. Down below he saw a red-haired boy crossing the street with a chicken on a string. He tried to force a smile.

Only an hour or so later came a report of the murder of a seamstress in the Faubourg St Antoine. He went out, cursing.

He dismounted from his horse with a sense of eternal recurrence. Another Crime, another Victim, and the expected Punishment merely a theoretical ideal of an ordered world. Ramon had his own opinions on such order. Was it justice, he asked himself, when he put a beggar in chains, or arrested some poor devil who had stolen vegetables from the priest's garden? Crime. Victim. Punishment. Was there justice for all? Or was justice variable? It was not a policeman's duty to define difficult concepts, he told himself, but simply to follow the law. 'Ah well, I'm not going to worry about it any more,' he resolved optimistically.

After questioning the woman's blind daughter and the staff and guests in the filthy pension next door without obtaining a single statement of any value whatsoever, he decided to visit all the sewing workshops on that side of the Seine, if for no other reason than to alleviate his own tension. At the same time he set three men to search Madame Arnault's room.

'Go through everything, from the stove to her stinking corsets,' he yelled at them as he left.

When he returned later in the afternoon they had found a promissory note among her papers. Back at the police station he discovered that it was identical with a document he himself had found among the possessions of the monk. It was the only clue they had, which he thought a good reason to take it seriously.

The following day he decided to go to Honfleur to interview the moneylender who had issued the promissory notes, a certain Bou-Bou Quiros.

It was spring in Honfleur and the hillside was covered in white apple-blossom. Ramon drank a glass of local calvados in a tavern before climbing the steep streets to the beautiful church of St Catherine. The young priest was able to give him the scanty information that the woman had died long before he himself had come to the town. Ramon went back to the tavern. An old boatbuilder mumbled something about a lawyer called Goupils having been the only one who knew her, and when Ramon bought him a calvados the address appeared on the table too.

Goupils' office was almost pathologically sparsely furnished. The lawyer himself was dressed expensively, but his office gave an impression of poverty. Ramon had to sit for some minutes on a hard wooden bench against the long wall before the lawyer deigned to raise his massively bewigged head from his account books. He said that Bou-Bou had died of natural causes, and professed ignorance of her business affairs in Paris, while admitting to their own business association with an expression of self-satisfaction typical of those who had enriched themselves from the labours and efforts of the poor. It was all quite convincing, yet it struck Ramon that he might be concealing something.

'Did she have any family?'

'No.'

A short pause.

'Except for a son.'

'A son?'

'Latour.'

'Maybe he would know something about it?'

'I doubt it. Anyway, he's hardly reliable.'

Goupils seemed suddenly embarrassed and rose from his desk. He adjusted his wig and began to stuff tobacco into his clay pipe with slow deliberate movements, staring down at his fingers as he did so.

'Where is the boy now?' Ramon asked.

Goupils lit his pipe, his chest gurgled and he had to hold his breath in order not to cough.

'Oh, I don't imagine he's still alive,' he croaked. 'He went off to Paris with one of Honfleur's flighty pieces. It would surprise me if he survived the journey.'

Goupils waved his arms dismissively as if to indicate that he wanted to resume work, but Ramon sat tight.

'This boy — did he help his mother with her business?'

'He wasn't even allowed near the account books! He was an untrustworthy thief.'

'Did he have any friends or acquaintances?'

Goupils cleared his throat impatiently.

'Inspector . . . I don't know what you're getting at with all these questions.'

He saw the detective before him, with his uncompromising eyes, and suddenly felt tired. He sat down again. Ramon stared resolutely into the lawyer's lined face and gradually the furrows seemed to quiver with memories. When he spoke again he sounded more cooperative and interested.

'What you must understand, Monsieur, is that the boy was a burden for his mother. She told me many times that she would like to be rid of him.'

'Her own son?'

'There was something solitary and naked about Latour. Like an empty room. All he had was Bou-Bou. He loved her too much. There was something excessive about his love.'

Goupils smiled to himself. When he addressed himself to Ramon again, it was as if a new thought had struck him.

'Even though he had the most ugly face imaginable, I've never been able to remember what he really looked like. I couldn't describe him for you. When he looked at his mother

I used to think his love would be the death of her. I think that was why she was afraid of him. Yes, that could have been it.'

'Is there anyone who might know what became of him?'

'The only people he talked to were Bou-Bou and an old taxidermist who lives in a hut right out in the woods. Otherwise he never said a word to anybody.'

Ramon stood on the quayside in Honfleur screwing up his eyes against the salt wind. He stood there for some time, letting his face be scoured clean by the wind before turning and walking back to the carriage. Having made the journey to Honfleur, he might as well do the job properly. He climbed in and asked the coachman to take him to the house of Léopold the taxidermist.

They only got as far as Regnault's land before Ramon had to leave the carriage and make his way on foot through the dense bushes to the little hut.

The taxidermist's face was the oldest Ramon had ever seen. It seemed almost ossified, chalky-white and ravaged, frozen in a grimace that was scrutinizing him carefully. A feeling of veneration came over him as he sat down on the stool opposite this ancient being. His parched features were turned towards Ramon, unmoving. His eyes were still piercing, his voice toneless and unemotional. Every word seemed to be an effort.

'I remember the boy well.'

He closed his eyes. Ramon wondered for a moment whether that was all he would get out of him, but then he seemed to collect himself and continued, 'He helped me here for several years. Strange boy, very bright, good with his hands. I think he saw himself as deformed but actually he just had rather puckered skin. He helped me here for several years. Very willing, almost obsequious, which used to infuriate me. But he was skilful with his hands, was little Latour.'

He sniffed and went quiet. Ramon didn't want to push him; he waited a while before asking, 'What happened to him?'

'Maybe I was too strict. He could be very irritating. He would smile when I told him off. At first I thought he was cheeky, then I realized he wanted me to throw him out or chastise him. But he was good with his hands, no doubt about that.'

The old man looked up at the animal heads around the walls, and Ramon followed his gaze, fascinated by the gleaming eyes.

'One day he didn't appear. It was only later I discovered what he'd done.'

'What, Monsieur?'

'He'd been into my library. Stolen books. Vesalius, Vieussens, my anatomical textbooks. Presents from the Royal Physician.'

The taxidermist looked at Ramon reproachfully, as if his old body were still weighed down by the disappointment.

*

Back in Paris Ramon gave further thought to the medical pamphlet he had read a few weeks earlier. He visited the Hôtel Dieu and the Medical Faculty buildings in the Rue de la Bûcherie to make enquiries among the students. But no one had heard of Latour-Martin Quiros, and Ramon was on the point of giving up when quite by chance he came upon Rouchefoucault's house nearby.

With some reluctance the servant showed him into the library. Rouchefoucault made him wait over half an hour before he strode in without any apology and grunted, 'What do you want?'

Ramon tried not to let his annoyance show as he explained his business. The professor's eyes lit up immediately.

'That young man. Where is he? Tell me where he is.'

Ramon shrugged his shoulders.

'I would love to know myself, professor.'

Rouchefoucault grunted in irritation again.

'Why are you here then, what do you want, why are you disturbing me in my work?'

Ramon explained as patiently as he could that this was a police investigation and that he wanted to speak to Quiros in connection with serious crimes.

But Rouchefoucault was clearly not interested in the Inspector's suspicions and went on to sing the praises of his former assistant. Ramon found this less than helpful and began to have doubts about the man's judgement. He might be a brilliant scientist but he seemed not to be greatly endowed with understanding of his fellow-men.

'Professor,' he interrupted, 'can you give me a description of this "Charles Cantin"?'

Rouchefoucault said that his assistant had protruberant eyes, and that his skull was a strange shape, indicating such characteristics as good memory, pride, love of authority, meticulousness, mimicry, sense of purpose and morality. He certainly had a great gift for anatomy, a retentive mind and displayed precision, dexterity and an uncommon devotion to his work. But beyond that the professor could not help. His assistant had toiled day and night, scarcely leaving the house. As far as he knew, he had no family, no friends or acquaintances, and he never spoke about personal matters. No, all in all he was an exceptionally reticent young man. At that point he paused, sucking on his lips.

'There was one thing,' he added, 'one thing that was very strange.'

Rouchefoucault's eyes took on an almost childlike appearance, and for the first time in the conversation he looked at Ramon with an air of bafflement.

'He never slept.'

'Not at all?'

'Well, I often wake up at night and make a note of things that occur to me, or put on an extra nightshirt and go out to the kitchen to drink some soup or a glass of wine. Every time I passed his door the light would be on, and he would be sitting at the window, quite motionless.'

Ramon gave him an enquiring look.

'One night I heard a crash out at the back. I went outside and found him on the ground. He'd fallen from the window and was lying in a heap on the stones. He was quite badly injured and bleeding from a gash in his forehead. Even now I can vividly recall bending over him and asking him whether he could move. He smiled up at me, the strangest smile I've ever seen, and said he couldn't feel anything. He actually sounded disappointed at not being even more injured.'

Ramon left Rouchefoucault's house in a disconsolate mood.

*

Latour lay on his bed at the inn. He could find no repose in this room; it still smelt of alcohol from the dissection and was a constant reminder of his failure. He had always believed that the organ for the sense of pain would be located next to the cerebellum. Rouchefoucault placed it between the organs for destructiveness, secrecy and aggression. But he had bungled the dissection. Madame Arnault had made him feel ill. As he cut into her brain in the semi-darkness of his lodgings his hands had shaken so much that he soon had a complete confusion of organs before him. He felt he was being observed, an intense gaze following his every movement. It was the 'watchful eye' that had made him ill.

184

He could not bear to be in that little room any longer. There was only one place he could think of to go.

He arrived at Madame de Sade's house early on a spring morning. He felt completely drained of energy and it was as much as he could do to knock on the door.

He was admitted by two grief-stricken women. Madame was grieving for the Marquis, and Gothon was grieving in sympathy. The household was deeply in debt, and Madame had had to dismiss several servants and sell paintings and furniture. There was a general air of dejection over the once splendid rooms.

She embraced him.

'Latour! We heard you had died of typhus.'

Latour drew back; he did not like such overwhelming displays of affection.

'I've nothing to offer you,' Madame Renée said once they were inside, looking down at the floor and pulling her shawl around her no longer youthful neck. Latour said he would be pleased to serve her even if she could not pay him.

'I am yours,' he said.

Madame thanked him, squeezing his hands so hard that he had trouble releasing them. As they proceeded along the dusty corridors to his old room, she told him about the feud between herself and her mother, and about the King's *lettre de cachet* written at the instigation of Madame de Montreuil that might keep the Marquis imprisoned for life. Renée had not been allowed to visit him since his arrest. Outside his door she paused and read him the Marquis' letter, clinging on to it as if it were a lifebuoy and reading every word as if it held a hidden meaning.

I am imprisoned in a tower behind nineteen iron doors. The only light that reaches me is through a pair of tiny windows with close-set bars. In the last two months I have only been let out for exercise five times. I am sitting in the dark, in a sort of tomb-chamber, surrounded by stone walls more than fifteen metres high . . .

She was crying.

'They censor his letters; he has to write in code. They punish him by taking away his pen and paper. You know how distraught he gets, Latour. It will affect his health if he remains in there. Tell me what to do.'

Latour withdrew to his room and when he locked the door he could imagine he heard it being locked on the outside too. He lay on his bed for days doing nothing. He felt so old. And he felt he had nothing in particular to live for.

He began to grieve too. He paced the floor, still feeling as if he was being observed. The 'watchful eye' was there the whole time. He put his hands up to his brow, crawled under the bed, didn't know what to do with himself. Whose eye was it? God's? What in Hell's name was it?

'Leave me in peace!' he yelled to the ceiling and to himself. Gothon came in search of comfort, but he sent her away. He was distressed whenever anybody set foot in his room, and convinced himself that it was not natural for anyone to cross the threshold. His profound anxiety made him shun his fellow-creatures.

Gothon returned and told him about a murderer prowling the streets of Paris. She sat on the side of his bed trembling as she spoke. The headless corpse of a woman had been found. Her incoherent chatter irritated Latour, and he sent her away again. He wanted to be alone.

A month or two after this he received via Renée a manuscript from the Marquis with an accompanying note asking him to make a fair copy of it. Latour, having always been

186

fascinated by the Marquis' writing, regarded it as a gift from heaven. He sat down at the desk and exchanged his anxieties for this new activity. He transcribed travelogues, comedies, sketches for novels, memoirs, letters, anecdotes. The Marquis' style was uneven, repetitive, ironical, didactic. He turned the world upside down. But Latour transformed his master's jottings into something finer, word by word, line by line and page by page, with the satisfaction experienced only by someone who felt he was at last getting the chance to atone for the wrongs he had committed.

*

Ramon sat with his eyes closed trying not to dwell on his conversation with the Prefect, the angry inquisitorial exchanges and his own arguments that had merely resulted in bringing him here, to this carriage and another pointless journey on police business. It was a torment and didn't bear thinking about. Yet for one reason or another he couldn't help but do so. His mind seemed to have an inbuilt need to keep going over the same painful episodes and draw nourishment from them like leeches. What good was such nourishment? Ramon didn't like the way the notions in his head seemed to have a life of their own but he didn't have the will to stop them. He felt trapped. After a new hearing in Aix Inspector Marais and some of his officers had stayed overnight at an inn with the prisoner. Marais trusted the Marquis de Sade and allowed him certain liberties. De Sade had abused that trust and escaped. Marais was raging; everyone was raging.

'I want you to go to La Coste, Ramon, and find De Sade. If he's not at the château, seize all of his delinquent writings. I want you to read them all, give me a summary of the contents and then destroy every single word. Understood?'

The Prefect had been white round the gills. Now Ramon was in a carriage on his way to Provence and cursing the day he started to work for d'Hémery. He cursed his own interest in literature and the fact that a writer and his ridiculous scribblings were diverting him from his case and taking precedence over murder.

He tried to convince himself that this was only a brief excursion, a short interlude in his investigations, and that his old routine would soon resume and he could continue his attempts to solve the sequence of crimes. But he was uneasy and decided to undertake this task with particular care and concern for detail. If he carried it out to perfection he might find it more meaningful, and it would satisfy his superiors and the injured feelings of that old misery Marais. The objections he had raised with the Prefect about being hot on the trail of the murderer still at large in Paris had been dismissed out of hand.

'And how long have you been hunting for this murderer?'

The Prefect's gruff irony. Ramon took solace in the thought that he had been put on this minor case because the honour of the police was at stake, and it was actually an honour for himself to be the one chosen to go to La Coste to sort it out. But nevertheless he spent the entire journey to Provence wishing he were back in Paris.

They were overtaken by rain, heavy rain, lashing the trees. The ditches flooded, roads and fields merging into one. Ramon kept exhorting the coachman but in the end he had to admit it was a waste of time and energy to attempt to continue, so they put up at an inn. Ramon lay listening to the rain all night.

By the time they arrived at the château, the Marquis had vanished. But they found piles of notebooks in his study. Novels, histories, plays, articles. Ramon had his two men transfer them all to the carriage, while he himself went over the whole building documenting the disarray of the rooms and the chaos in the kitchen, as if to prove that he had searched for the Marquis in every tiny corner.

In one room he found some objects that made him feel sick: a crucifix and a cupboard full of instruments of torture: whips, tongs, handcuffs. They inspired in him such a morbid fascination that he forgot to list them. What was it about pain that so attracted people? What was it that made a man like De Sade devote his life to the pursuit of pain? And then it occurred to him that the only thing that could make a person do anything so absurd was love. Without taking a single note he rushed out of the room, sought out his men and harangued them to work faster.

As soon as he arrived back in Paris he decided to read all the Marquis' ramblings as quickly as he could. To have done with them, to be able to return to his case and solve it. He ploughed through page after page of longwinded prose, rising from his desk at intervals to walk about the room as if to shake off potential infection. He tried to convince himself that the notebooks had been given him as a trial by God. If he couldn't get through this, the hundreds of pages in writing as laboriously tortuous as the actions it described, he would not be up to solving his case. He bit on his pen; then stood up and spat out of the window.

Farewell, decency! Farewell, honour! Rousseau, Voltaire, listen to this! When you talk about virtue, when you talk about reason and high ideals, when you say that goodness is the only path to happiness, you are wrong. What you should have shown us was virtue overcome by cruelty. That way you would have held the reader's interest. Yes, show us a woman raping her son; killing him; sending her own mother to the gallows; marrying

189

her own father. But you daren't. You cannot. Because
you haven't enough talent to see that nature is a cruel
machine. No, in your petty works there is nothing of
such truth. Your sensitivity and decency are false.
Measured against the genius of Monsieur de Sade you
are nothing but shadows. Adieu!

Ramon continued reading and thought he was not taking it in
properly. He could not remember the little story he had just
finished: his thoughts must have strayed. Though he had read
every word, his mind must have been on his own case as he did
so, because De Sade's story could hardly be about what he
thought he had just read. He stopped, closed his eyes for a
moment. This was a test and would soon be over. It was absurd
to lose your mind because of a writer. He sat up straight and
turned back the pages, concentrated hard and began again. The
same thing happened: the same story repeated. The realization
dawned on him that this was not confusion: he had in front of
him a text that could solve the mystery of his murderer's identity.

He read some of the passages once more.

I could get no answers to my innumerable questions. The
minister's pleasures were too intense.

'Mademoiselle,' cried the minister, my lover, beckon-
ing me closer. He was fondling the bishop's arse while he
whipped an old woman suspended by a rope from the
ceiling. The bishop was inserting his prick into the anus
of young Rosaria. The minister handed me a whip.

'Let yourself go, my dear, don't hold anything back.
Let pleasure be your sole pursuit, let nothing be as as
holy as pleasure.'

I whipped him. I humiliated him and tortured him with
a smile on my face. And later I let the men do with me
whatever they wanted, as long as they treated me as a

common whore. The further I sank into degradation, the deeper into shame, the greater was the excitement, the arousal and the violence of my ecstasy.

The next morning I walked through the forest in this foreign land, letting the mountain breeze cool my sore limbs. As I came to a small grove of trees I caught sight of something that astonished me. Dear reader, you know by now that I am no stranger to the excesses of cruelty or the pleasure to be had from the simplest acts. But the scene I now witnessed, involuntarily and by chance, shook me to the core of my being.

A diminutive figure in a tricorn hat was bending over a man who was tied to four stakes fixed in the ground. The victim's tongue had been excised and was lying beside him, and only the faintest gurgling sounds were emanating from his throat. The little man had a scalpel in his hand and was quietly and methodically decapitating him.

I saw the victim twisting this way and that, desperate to die. Death was reflected in the face of his executioner. I stood frozen to the spot in the undergrowth. I dared not move. The little man kept him alive for almost an hour. In the midst of all this evil he remained unbelievably calm. He seemed to be relishing what he was doing, giving little cries of delight from time to time. He was totally engrossed, intoxicated by the joy of cruelty. Finally with an adroit movement he cut through the neck and then across the head from ear to ear and pulled the skin down over the face of the still-living victim. Then he began to dissect the man's brain . . .

I went home, and packed my things in complete silence. I left this foreign land and the minister, knowing that I had to forget everything I had seen and heard and devote myself to virtue.

The description was too close to the murderer's *modus operandi* to be coincidence. Ramon sprang up from his desk. 'As long as I go carefully,' he thought, 'I've got him, and I won't rest until I've caught him.'

*

After a month of freedom the Marquis was arrested at La Coste. Ramon was waiting for him in cell number six in Vincennes Prison when the warders led him in. The Inspector was admiring the view from the prison window, the moat and the trees surrounding the white buildings of the prison itself. It was very beautiful. The Marquis starting bawling at him immediately, shouting obscenities and flailing his arms.

'I was freed by the court in Aix. Yet I'm sent back here. Why? Because of one mad cow, Madame la Présidente, and an equally idiotic *lettre de cachet*. What Piron said about the Académie Française could just as well apply to this clique: *There they sit, forty of them, with the intelligence of four.*'

The Marquis puffed out his chest, gesticulated, made faces — but Ramon had made up his mind not to succumb to provocation.

'I'll never forgive the people responsible for holding me here without good legal grounds, and the most shameful part of it, the worst thing of all, Inspector, is that they can't even tell me when I'll be released or *whether* I'll be released. It's irrational and it's inhumane. It's brutal. They're bloody torturers!'

Ramon nodded indulgently. When the Marquis finally calmed down and took a seat at the table, out of breath, Ramon drew up the chair opposite him, extracted the little story from his jacket pocket and laid it on the table.

'Are you familiar with this?'

The Marquis gave the text a cautious glance and looked up at Ramon in scorn.

'Certainly I am. I wrote it myself. You must have stolen it from me and now you're restoring it to me. Very kind of you. You can go now, and think yourself lucky that your crime, which is worse than mine, will be regarded with a modicum of humanity. I shall not report you. Good day to you.'

Ramon gave a caustic smile.

'Let us make a deal. If you tell me the truth behind this story I'll do everything in my power to get you out of here.'

The Marquis spat on the floor.

'When I first arrived here everyone said it wouldn't be more than three months at most. They would do "everything in their power" to get me released. After two years they said "it won't be more than three years". Now they say nothing. Silence. Tell me what these brutes hope to gain by keeping my release date a secret. Can't they see that it's unjust and that they won't turn me into a better person by locking me up? Don't they know that I won't be able to endure such treatment?'

Ramon avoided the intensity of the Marquis' gaze and looked round the cell instead, at all the books, papers, medicines.

'Monsieur de Sade, I've read your writings, plays, histories, novels, the lot. They're the most repulsive things I've ever seen. If you care so much about inhumanity and injustice, why do you write so immorally?'

The Marquis put his head on one side and mimicked the Inspector's spurious bonhomie.

'My dear Inspector, aren't prison, the daily infringements of human dignity, the backbiting, the incompetence, the methodical inhumanity that permeates the whole country's legal system proof of the fact that I am right? I think I give a faithful picture of the world.'

'You encourage cruelty.'

'I have summoned up in my imagination almost every aspect of a life of libertinism, but that does not mean I have put it all into practice. It's an essential feature of writing, Inspector, to distinguish between fact and fiction. I've never been an angel, but my crimes are ridiculously petty in comparison with those perpetrated on a daily basis by those who govern and administer the country.'

'Excuses.'

'I didn't expect you to understand.'

'If you are such an opponent of injustice, tell me who the murderer is in this story you've written. Who was it who took the life of this innocent person?'

He met the Marquis' eyes now and thought he could detect him beginning to waver.

'It's a fictional character.'

'It is not a fictional character. The murderer kills in a very specialized way and obviously has a knowledge of anatomy and dissection. I've investigated five murders in Paris all committed in exactly the same manner. It's the same person responsible for all of them, and the same kind of murder you described here. It really happened.'

The Marquis made no reply, but Ramon felt certain he knew the murderer's identity.

'Tell me who he is.'

'No.'

'You might make me think it was you yourself.'

'You know it wasn't me.'

Ramon straightened up.

'How can you defend someone who kills another?'

'I don't have to defend him.'

Ramon leaned across the table.

'Help me. Help yourself. Tell me how I can find this man. Make sure he receives his punishment and doesn't kill again.

It would be insane, can't you see, insane not to help me?'

'Tell me why I should believe in the system of justice in France. Get me out of here, give me even the slightest reason to believe that you're all fair and just, and then I'll help you. But keep me locked up like an animal, like a mad dog, torment me and torture me every single hour of the day with your silence, and I'll repay silence with silence.'

Ramon stood up from the table in such a rage of impotence that the chair tipped over and crashed to the stone floor.

The gates of the prison opened, and he went out into the night. He stormed across the grass towards the carriage but suddenly came to a halt under the trees, turning and looking back at the majestic Château de Vincennes and its white tower, trying to make out where the Marquis' cell number six would be. 'I'll get the better of you,' he thought, cool and clear-headed again. 'You'll tell me the truth if I have to use the oldest method of all and Article 164 of 1539. If I have my way, you'll be strapped to the torture bench, and the flames will lick you till you talk.'

But sitting in his room, looking out into the darkness and listening to the sounds of a disturbance a few streets away, he realized he was allowing himself to be affected by the mind of another person. The fury he had felt as he left Vincennes was that of a murderer, not his own.

He arrived at Madame de Sade's house early the next morning. He sat talking to her for a long time, but she was extremely unwilling to give him any information. When he asked whether she knew the name Latour-Martin Quiros, she shook her head. When he asked again whether her husband had ever known such a person, she said she had never heard of anyone by that name. Ramon explained to her how serious the matter was and in the end he showed her the story De Sade had written. He had expected her to be shocked and upset, but she read it calmly. When she put it down she had only a few literary comments to make and pointed out some grammatical infelicities. Ramon told her he believed De Sade had actually witnessed the murder, but she merely shrugged her shoulders.

He went to De Sade's lawyer, Gaufridy, who was more willing to talk about the Marquis' circle of acquaintances. But he knew no one of that name either. It could have been one of De Sade's many servants or footmen, he said.

From Madame de Montreuil, Ramon received confirmation that the Marquis had a footman named Latour. But the shrewish little woman declared that he had died of typhus.

It was with mixed emotions that Inspector Ramon informed the head of the Sûreté that he wished to close the case.

6

The Electric Man

I heard every word the Inspector said. I saw Madame Renée's tense face through the kitchen doorway, the policeman's fingers leafing through the papers.

How can I describe my sensations?

It was like falling again, like falling through the air. I saw the policeman's lips forming the words in the story the Marquis had written:

'. . . *the scene I now witnessed, involuntarily and by chance, shook me to the core of my being.*'

I was near to retching.

'*The little man had a scalpel in his hand and was quietly and methodically decapitating him.*'

I knelt down in a corner of the kitchen and was violently sick.

Later, lying in bed, I considered the possibility of leaving France. Perhaps I could continue my work in Italy. But I was unable even to leave the room. I ran my hands over my body. My limbs were stiff. I pinched myself. My belly came out in red blotches.

I closed my eyes but couldn't sleep. I saw the Count in my mind's eye, on his chestnut stallion, myself running after him through the forest, catching up with him in open country. I remembered the stakes, the scalpel, the nerve fibres, the sun going down. And there in among the trees must have been the Marquis. His eyes concealed in the undergrowth. His eyes. The mysterious watchful eyes that had pursued me everywhere since and made me ill.

The meadow near Chambéry is a sacrificial site. I certainly sacrificed something there. The mere thought of the Marquis' gaze made me go cold all over.

I did not sleep for four days. My head was full of recurring images: the Count, the Count's horse, the scalpel, the nerve fibres, the stakes, the trees, the eyes. On the fifth day I left my room, went out to the woodshed, picked up the axe and put my hand on the chopping block. I stared down at my pale, effeminate hand. I had always been so competent with my hands. My left hand was on the block. I raised the axe. Would I feel pain now? I looked from my hand to the axe and back again. Then I brought the axe crashing down with all my might.

Blood cascaded all over the block, splashing on to my trousers. My hand fell to the ground in front of me, my fingers still twitching. A wave of giddiness. My left arm was completely without feeling, hanging limply at my side. I was numb, but there was no pain. The ground began to move beneath me — and then I collapsed.

When I regained consciousness, the doctor had already treated me: my wrist was tightly bandaged. Renée and Gothon were at my side, looking tall and awkward. They didn't know what to say and simply repeated to me what the doctor had said. I listened with a smile on my lips. They mentioned the risk of gangrene and the need to change the dressing twice a day and told me it would soon start to hurt. I smiled at them. That night I slept without thinking of the meadow or the stakes.

Gothon came in to see me one morning and seemed touch-ingly concerned. She sat down on the side of the bed and chattered nervously about nothing in particular. Then she asked me about my hand and what had happened. I said it was an accident. She was silent for a moment.

'An accident?'

I smiled at her.

The Marquis' letters were arriving more frequently. Madame would come to my room and read them aloud to me, as if she believed that would alleviate her loss.

He protested his innocence. He admitted being too fond of women, of being guilty of seduction and debauchery of the lewdest kind and so forth. 'I am a libertine,' he wrote, 'but I am neither a criminal nor a murderer.'

What could I say? His words were all I had.

After some time in prison the Marquis was starting to become confused. He began writing strange combinations of numbers: 8, 15, 23. Was there any significance in them? Some kind of countdown to the day of his release? Or were they a reference to what had happened in Savoy? It seemed to me they might be, but I didn't want an answer. I could never ask what he had really seen, but I could look for clues in his letters.

I engrossed myself in the notebooks he had sent me. I submerged myself in an ocean of words.

As I re-wrote the manuscripts I stopped thinking about the eyes. Writing offered a kind of respite. I wrote his words and felt he was no longer able to see me. I knew we had a secret understanding.

My hair had gone completely grey. Just in the course of a few weeks. Did I miss the black colour? No, I didn't miss it, it was a relief to be rid of it. I liked grey.

I spent my time poring over the Marquis' manuscripts, the hours passing unnoticed. I had no desire to go out. Sitting at my desk I was clear-headed, motivated and knew exactly what I was doing. Gothon and Madame tried to divert me with their feminine wiles, tried to gain access to the Marquis through me, but this was my celibacy, my voluntary prison.

I received letters from the Marquis telling me what corrections to make or when to begin a new work. Every time I opened another letter I momentarily wondered whether it might contain the story from Savoy. Though I suspected that would never come.

From time to time the prison authorities prohibited the Marquis from writing, and then the manuscripts were smuggled out on thin numbered rolls of paper. I was often completely at a loss as to what belonged where. But I never wrote back. I corrected and improved the text according to my own judgement, and whenever I felt the Marquis had made the written construct itself into a prison, with sentences resembling endless walls, oppressive adjectives and moat-like paragraphs that went in circles round a walled-up plot, I opened up a little hole in the text to let in some air. It was my way of conversing with my master.

I was not unhappy in my self-imposed incarceration. Perhaps I was even content. The Marquis' drafts of his novels became a part of me. They were scraps and fragments, pieces of dialogue; malice and provocation, perverse sexuality, destructiveness. All norms of behaviour inverted. An immense darkness seemed to cast its shadow over the words. The darkness ate into me, but I didn't mind, because the Marquis was a great thinker.

I went to Gothon's room and asked her to forget that I had sent her away. She was in a bad mood and turned her back on me. But she let me in eventually to spend the night with her.

She was kind, a chambermaid with a typically Swiss plumpness and a sloping forehead, a sign of stubbornness. She was as childlike as ever, even though now worn out and wrinkled and grey-haired. I laid my head on her rotund belly, listened to her unfinished incoherent sentences and fell asleep. I had never understood Gothon.

When I woke up she was stroking the stump of my arm.

'There are so many things about you that remind me of the master,' she said. 'Your voices are so alike . . .'

Our voices were totally dissimilar.

'I hear there have been storms in La Coste. Do you think the château could be in ruins? . . . The poor Marquis . . . Latour . . . People say the strangest things about him . . . You . . . you were so often so alike . . .'

I covered her mouth with my hand and pushed her down on to the bed. She smiled.

'Yes, why don't you do away with me?'

'Don't be absurd,' I replied.

I went to her room the next night and drew on her with my quill pen. She moaned in ecstasy. But my flesh was weak, and I couldn't make love to her.

Now and again I took out the old anatomy books, Vesalius and Vieussens. Read a few sections here and there. I looked up my own notes from my time with Rouchefoucault and from my own investigations. I added a few paragraphs, but it was all too incomplete; there was still so much yet to discover.

I received more drafts of new novels from the Marquis. Descriptions of orgies so degenerate that they made my stomach heave. I struggled with his sentences. But with every vile utterance, every blasphemous oath and every base act that was committed on the wretched victims, I felt better. The cruelty became unreal, and I began to perceive that it was not the pleasure in these activities that the Marquis was trying to describe: it was loneliness. The desert of isolation. The emptiness of his prison. The stories were about pain: the body's pain was the only proof that his isolation was not total. Was that why I could feel no pain?

Could there be any significance in the fact that I would never feel pain? Could I put that gap in my experience to any use?

*

I stood in the doorway of Madame's room. There was a candle flickering on her bedside table next to a dish of plums. She had unfastened her dress at the back and her bare shoulder was towards me. She turned and we stared at each other.

'Did you call, Madame?'

'No.'

'I heard your voice.'

'It must have been somebody else.'

'There's no one else here, Madame.'

'Well, I don't want anything.'

'But you called.'

'No.'

'You wouldn't want to refuse me anything, Madame?'

'Go to your room, Latour. Are you drunk?'

'We've done a lot for each other.'

'What do you mean?'

'If the Marquis was ever unable to fulfil his duties, I carried them out for him. I was often him, and he was me.'

'Don't touch me, Latour.'

'My little piglet, my angel, my moon-cat. I know all the endearments he used for you. My Lolotte. Take off your dress, Renée. Lie over the bed. I'll go into the tightest part of you. I'll only hurt you a little.'

But I just stood there looking at her, aware of my vain boasts and awkward gestures. I took a step towards her, and she looked at me in amazement. Seizing her by the shoulder and forcing her down on the bed, my courage failed me, and I dropped to the floor, kneeling abjectly before her.

'Forgive me, Madame.'

I held her ankle and raised her foot to my lips and kissed it. She smiled and stroked my hair, caressed my head. I gently lifted her petticoat and kissed her hairy legs. Behind her knee, where it smelt sweetly of sweat, and the skin was damp. I bit her lightly on the kneecap and, breathing more heavily now, began to kiss her along the inside of her thigh. Her skin was soft and smooth, and there were dark hairs all the way up her thigh to her groin. She stood up and took off her clothes. She rose tall above me, nicely rounded, with breasts of unequal size and protruding hipbones. Her navel was like a dark eye. I put my tongue into it, and she sighed, but it sounded more like a groan caused by constipation than the panting of desire. I moved up and nibbled her breasts as if they were apples, nibbled at them as I ran my hand over her sweaty back. She tasted of sweat, but that only excited me more. I had difficulty keeping still. She stroked my head again, and I sucked at her dank vagina.

After a while she ordered me to do what the Marquis used to do, and what I'd had in mind from the first. She lay on her stomach over the bed, and I rubbed my prick slowly back and forth between her buttocks. I lubricated her with spittle. My breath was rhythmic as a song. Finally I pushed into her anus. I cried out. She cried out. We sang together. It was a false melody rising above our ugly bodies, our straining movements, rising out through the window, through the streets, into the park, across the town, towards a white prison and a cell number six, where a lonely man sat in the semi-darkness, leaning over a roll of parchment and covering it with writing.

For the first time in months I succeeded in leaving the house. I wandered about at random. Put up at an inn by the town wall. Slept without dreaming. In the morning I began my search. I found the tannery owner, Jean Foubert. Number seven. I watched him come out of the tannery with two apprentices. He was a corpulent man with sturdy arms and legs, a low brow and deepset eyes. His neck was thick and powerful. I followed his carriage until it came to a stop outside a little red house. Which he went into. He lived alone. But I didn't dare go in after him; instead I sat in a tree and waited, deep in thought. When dusk fell, I climbed down and returned to Madame de Sade's house. Back in my own room I vowed that I would never dissect again.

I worked hard on the Marquis' manuscripts. One morning Madame brought me a letter, without meeting my eyes, and said in her reedy voice, 'A letter for Martin Quiros. From Vincennes Prison.'

With that she was gone. My hand trembled as I broke the seal. I began reading the Marquis' dense writing and found the letter to have a cheery tone.

> *Martin Quiros . . . You've been a naughty boy! If I were there I would give you a beating . . . I would pluck off that smart toupee of yours that I know you renew every year with horsehair from a nag on the Paris to Courtheson road. And what would you do then?*
>
> *Monsieur Quiros . . . My cares and woes are diminishing. Thanks to my great protector, Madame la Présidente de Montreuil, I hope to be able to express my greetings*

in person, Martin Quiros, the day after tomorrow — in five years' time. Were my fate connected with any other family, I might have remained here for ever. For as you know, my friend, lack of respect for prostitutes does not go unpunished. Say what you will about governments, the King, religion, and it means nothing. But as for a prostitute, take care when you insult her if you don't want to raise the ire of all the police and judges and Montreuils and pillars of the brothels in her defence. They fearlessly lock up even the nobility for twelve or fifteen years. For the sake of a whore. Nothing is more wonderful than the French police! If you have a sister, a cousin or a daughter, Monsieur Quiros, advise her to become a whore. You would have to go a long way to find a more respected profession . . .

I also have my little indulgences, and even if they are not perhaps as exciting as yours, they are no less subtle. I walk up and down, and to entertain me at table I have a man who — and I do not exaggerate — takes ten pinches of snuff, sneezes six times, wipes his nose, spits and coughs at least fourteen times, all within the course of half an hour. Does that seem to you suitable relaxation? You know that my pleasures are on a par with yours, Quiros. But while yours degrade you, mine lead to virtue. Ask Madame de Montreuil if there is anything better in the whole world than lock and key to lead a man along the path of virtue. I am well aware there are monsters — like your good self (please excuse me) — who maintain that you should try prison once, and if it doesn't have any effect it's pointless trying it again. Such a view is a great mistake, Señor Quiros. This is how the argument should go: Prison is the only cure we know in France, so prison cannot be anything but good; and since prison is good, it

should be used in every case. And if it is not successful
the first time, then try, try, try again . . . Bleeding is good
for fever; we know of no better cure in France. Bleeding
is marvellous. But, Quiros, a patient with bad nerves or
thin blood is hardly likely to benefit from bleeding; a
different cure has to be found. 'Not at all,' the doctor
snorts, 'bleeding is excellent, it's been proved. Monsieur
Quiros has a fever and so he must be bled regardless.'
That is seen as a decisive argument.

Oh, Quiros my son, how intelligent we are in this cen-
tury of ours!

What bitter irony there was in all this. The Marquis was
jailed for his way of making love, but there must have been
hundreds of far more wicked characters on the loose in Paris
who had committed worse crimes. The Marquis was ill and
unhappy. I ought to have wept.

I should have gone to the police and confessed. Before they
executed me, I could turn to God and beg for a punishment
that would make me feel pain. In Hell pain would free me
from the person who had lived under the name of Latour,
from all his thoughts and memories. Forgetfulness would be
sublime. All thoughts would be erased in pain. But then it
occurred to me that God's punishment might be far worse. I
might be admitted to Paradise and sit among the angels on
soft cloud cushions without feeling any pain. I would yearn
for pain every single hour of the day and yet still never be able
to experience it.

Gothon returned from her cousin in Orléans and I spent
several nights in her care. When she heard about the letter I
had received from the Marquis but which I refused to let her
read, her eyes were sorrowful. I knew then that it was Gothon's
affection for her master that had been transferred to me, and

that it was her master's hand she worshipped, so to speak, not mine. But that didn't bother me. I loved seeing her sink down on the bed and look up at me with an expression already intoxicated by the little pain she knew was about to come. I suffered no anxiety or nightmares.

But my old anxiety recurred as autumn approached. Everything was awry. The price of bread, reversals of fortune in the war with England, my master's letters full of sarcasm and his morbid obsession with numbers. Renée and Madame de Montreuil were arguing more than ever. The Royal Decree relating to imprisonment was immutable. Madame was desolate. And Gothon was no longer an angel of goodwill; she had become bitter and surly and had started praying with Madame and accompanying her to church. I was oppressed by this quasi-life: it was nothing but a shadow of how life used to be. I was irritable, as if waiting for something, but with no idea of what it was likely to be.

I read through my anatomical notes and could not help concluding that I had made a serious error, though I really could not fathom how.

I saw in a newspaper that the young balloonist Pilâtre de Rozier had attempted a crossing of the English Channel from Boulogne. A huge crowd gathered at the coast and watched the balloon climb to a height of fifteen hundred metres before bursting into purple flames with an indescribable explosion. Rozier and his companion were thrown out, and their bodies shattered when they hit the ground, limbs flying in all directions. They said even his head was torn from his body. In the newspaper report Rozier was described as a 'martyr to science'. I was very depressed about it, having keenly followed his fabulous inventions. He was a man of the new age, and this mishap was a setback for the whole country.

*

When Renée was finally granted permission to visit the Marquis in Vincennes Prison, after four years of refusal, the poor woman was castigated for having been unfaithful. The Marquis was in such a rage that the authorities immediately called a halt to her visits. His accusations so filled her with despair that she decided to leave the house and enter the Convent of Sainte-Aure to prove her fidelity. Gothon and I were left alone in the enormous house that was crumbling into ruin around us.

I continued transcribing the manuscripts, but the work was getting harder and harder.

It was the Marquis' way of tyrannizing me. Even in prison he exerted his control over me. He was trying to make my thoughts his own, his writing mine. He was suffering in prison and trying to live through me. I would not go along with it.

I decided to put the manuscripts aside. I went to Gothon's room, slipped into her bed and pressed up against her warm body the way I used to. But she didn't respond; she just went on sleeping. She was getting old now. She had been born the same year as myself. Her grey hair and the folds of her belly made me aware of my own age. I pinched her — she used to like being woken with a little sting of pain — but she just rolled over.

I was suddenly certain of something I had suspected for a long time: Gothon was ill. Her misty eyes and constant belching were unmistakable signs. She was sick but was trying to hide it from me. Why, what had I done wrong?

'Do you feel unwell?' I asked. But she just looked away,

refused to answer, lines of pain at the corners of her mouth. Her silence made me angry.

I went to Sainte-Aure and asked Madame.

'Gothon cannot bear the thought of others worrying about her or feeling sorry for her,' she said. 'I think she would rather suffer in silence. You have to remember that the greater part of her life has been spent sinning with men. Now she wants to be alone.'

I walked the streets as if in a daze. Why hadn't she said anything to me? She was dying, and everyone knew, even the Marquis from behind his thick walls, but I had had no inkling at all. She was suffering, and I knew nothing. I went up to her room when I got back and found her lying in bed with her eyes half open, looking up at me strangely. I didn't want to be angry but I could feel my temper getting the better of me.

'Are you ill?'

She shook her head. I tried to control my exasperation.

'You're not telling the truth.'

She sat up in bed.

'I'll only tell you what I want to tell you.'

'Why do you pretend you can't see me?'

'Because I want to be left in peace.'

'Do you think you're dead already? Is that why you don't say anything to me? Have you lost your tongue? Or your mind?'

She was different, no longer her old self. Why was she treating me like this? Hadn't I always been good to her? I went over to her and hit her. Her lip started to bleed, but she didn't bow her head. She didn't apologize, she didn't say what I hoped she would say. She didn't lay her warm hand on my forehead. She made a fist and hit me back.

'Now I'll never tell you.'

'That must really please you.'

'I want to be left alone. I've never liked you, Latour. You make me feel worse. Leave me in peace!'

I moved out of the house.

Paris was uninviting, cold and dirty, the people pale and downtrodden. I rented a room from a wine merchant in the Faubourg Saint-Marcel. It was on the fourth floor, cheap and correspondingly dilapidated. I lay in the disgusting bed and dreamt disgusting dreams. There was an entire family living in the adjacent room, and a constant stream of invective was audible through the wall. Two emaciated whores shared the room above, and were running up and down stairs all day and all night. I watched them from my half-open door, and they gave me contemptuous looks. I closed my eyes and let my imagination take over. I was woken by a cool fresh breeze blowing in through the window.

The house of the tannery owner was in darkness. I felt in fine form. I had my implements in my hand, and it was no problem at all to silence the guard dog. I entered by the back stairs. It was pitch dark inside and smelt of rancid cheese and wine. I took off my shoes and made my way to the bedroom. The tannery owner was not a quiet sleeper: I could hear him snoring. I stood over him and noticed his fetid breath. His deep nostrils were vibrating. Only when I brought out my scalpel, put on my one glove and made ready to start did I realize how weak I was. The weight of the scalpel in my hand was ridiculous. I was sweating. It felt so preposterously heavy that it pushed my hand down towards the floor. I was forced to my knees, fighting against the weight of a scalpel. The man grunted in the bed above me, just as if he were mocking me.

He died from a clumsy stab in the neck. As a scientist I was totally inept.

I left my filthy room. I sat in a park, frost in the air, freezing cold, rocking back and forth on a bench, my breath vapourizing in front of me. I tried to curb my terrible fantasies, tried to think of Gothon, her warm hands and soft mouth. I tried to make myself get up and walk through the park to the house to see her before it was too late. But I stayed on the bench, I was so cold, hardly able to keep my eyes open, I fell asleep, my wild fantasies beginning again, cities of blood rising up before me, knives in my hands, the doors of the houses were human bodies that I had to cut open to get into the warmth. When I awoke, it was dusk. A full moon. A windless evening. I stood up and went back to the house. But there was no one there. A neighbour told me that Gothon had gone to the convent to be with her mistress. When I arrived at Saint-Aure I knew she was dead.

I could see her face through the doorway. She was lying on the bed with the cover up to her sagging throat. Her eyes were closed, her mouth half open. Renée was sitting beside her leaning her head against the wall, praying. A candle flickered on the bedside table between them. Renée turned and looked at me with bright pious eyes. I wept.

I sat in Renée's room all night, staring at the wall, my mind blank. Towards morning I fell asleep. When I woke up I was extremely hot and couldn't move. My legs had no feeling in them. A nun came to take care of me. They carried me to a guest room. When I attempted to stand up, my legs gave way, and I couldn't walk. The Mother Superior was worried that my stump might be infected. They gave me herb tea to drink.

The whole room smelt like a cloister garden.

*

The feeling gradually returned to my legs. Madame persuaded the Mother Superior to allow me to stay in the overgrown gardener's cottage at the bottom of the convent garden. For a while. Until I was well again. That brief period extended, thanks to Madame Renée's tenacity, into several years. I was well liked by the nuns.

So I lay sleeping in this little stone house with its narrow bed and desk, candle, crucifix and Bible. I only woke up to drink and eat some bread and then I would lie down again. I had no dreams and when I lay awake I felt numb and intoxicated by sleep. Just thinking about my anatomical experiments made me lethargic. I was in a kind of torpor.

When my legs had recovered, I started doing some gardening. I was really keen to do it. I could only walk slowly after the paralysis, but it didn't prevent me working.

The nuns were very fond of me.

I loved the job, and the friendliness of the nuns meant a lot. I read of the unrest throughout the country from the occasional newspaper that found its way into the convent, but not a word about the 'Anatomist'. So everything had gone according to plan. But I was not particularly bothered about it. I didn't really want to think about it. It all seemed such a very long time ago. Was I getting old?

Everywhere was so quiet. Never before had I experienced such silence. I was completely relaxed there, no thoughts to torment me, no eyes watching me.

It was in that haven of prayer and atonement that I received the first draft of the Marquis' *120 Days of Sodom*.

In the index I came across the name of the Président de Curval.

It seemed as if that fictional man had been pursuing me my whole life long. I put the manuscript down. Hadn't I finished with all that? Wasn't it behind me now? Hadn't I made a fresh start? I sat by the window and looked out over the herb garden. Parsley, thyme. I hoped it would rain soon — it would do the garden good.

I picked up the manuscript again and continued reading avidly.

> *Président de Curval had been one of the pillars of society. Now he was sixty and bore all the signs of his dissolute life. He was tall and as dry and thin as a skeleton. His eyes were joyless. He was as hairy as a satyr. His buttocks were flabby, hanging down like a pair of dirty rags between his thighs. The flesh was so tough and dead, thanks to the countless lashes of the whip it had experienced, that you could knead it like dough without his feeling a thing. In the centre between his buttocks — and it was not necessary to splay them to see it — was a hole of such vast diameter that its size, smell and colour were more reminiscent of some fearful privy than of a human arse . . .*

I closed the manuscript up.

I went down to the forest, as far as the sparkling river. I took off my clothes and stared at my own reflection in the water.

My body was beginning to get quite shrivelled.

120 Days of Sodom. The monstrous blasphemy of the words seemed intensified within the holy walls of the convent. The episodes were sexually macabre and infinitely repetitive. The same things occurred again and again. Children and pregnant women were tortured to death, libertines ate excrement and entertained one another with stories of incest and parental murder. Events that took place in the enclosed world of the château were a microcosm of a sick era, I thought. There were no values any more. Women turned into men, and men into women, evil was good and good evil, and God was the greatest sinner of all. Lust was the sole driving force people had, and lust inevitably led to death.

I tried not to think of the Président de Curval, and never finished reading the description of him. Half way through the manuscript I suddenly knew I could not continue with it. I no longer understood what I was copying. I wanted to change whole passages to make them meaningful.

One morning I decided to go to the Mother Superior and ask if I could speak to her. She received me in her spartan office. Once I began to speak, I couldn't stop. I said I felt duty-bound to serve the Marquis. I explained my feelings of love for him. I became flustered. I stumbled over my words. I said things I didn't mean. I lied and made excuses, yet everything I said was also true. The Mother Superior looked at me as if she understood. She didn't repudiate me when I confessed to having sinned most heinously, nor when I said I had only now come to realize that I had used the ideas of great men to justify the results of my own menial activities. When I eventually came to a halt she stood up and said, 'You don't need my advice, my son.'

All that day and the night that followed I sat by the river, deep in thought. Rouchefoucault. De Sade. My experiments. Pain, the controlling organ of pain. *120 Days of Sodom.* Gothon. Madame de Sade. And the Mother Superior.

In the morning I went back to my cottage and began to write. My confessions.

I wrote about the three great men under whom I had studied: Léopold, Rouchefoucault, De Sade. Three masters of anatomy, science and literature. And I wrote of the way I had abused the knowledge and honourable intentions of these masters. After a pause for thought, I wrote, very slowly now, almost as if my hand were losing its strength, that I had been in love with the pain of others. There I stopped and tore up all the sheets I had written and went out and burnt them and dug the ashes into the soil. Then I returned to my desk and began all over again. And wrote exactly the same things. I stared down at my words and realized that they were far more frightening than I was. What I read seemed to have been written by another person, but *about me*. 'What a spineless wretch this Latour-Martin Quiros must have been,' I thought, 'so heartless.' Yet after only a few pages the same spinelessness and heartlessness sounded like something magnificent, perhaps because it was written and had taken on a value that was higher than reality? Finally I described how my curiosity about pain had become so fatally entwined with scientific research . . .

Having completed my introduction, I packed up the Marquis' manuscript together with as much of the transcription as I had completed and sent it to the Bastille. It did not bring a sense of relief. I could not believe I had done it and for the next few days felt very apprehensive.

Sometimes I thought I wanted to leave Paris for ever. To settle in some remote place where there were hardly any people. Where I could try to finish my confessions.

I often took my notebooks with me and went outside to write in the mild spring night. I didn't find it too depressing to strip my life's work of all the dignity I had previously ascribed to it. It was liberating to be able to view oneself as if from a great distance. It was as if I said: *I was clearly a monster.* It felt like a privilege. It was as if I were no longer myself when I wrote. So by providing moral advice for others not to follow in my footsteps I was able to give my life some significance. I wrote about my mother, about Honfleur, about Léopold, about the tiger we stuffed; I even described how I, the ugly and jealous child, tried to kill my mother's lover. By daybreak I had burnt three candles; I went for a morning dip in the river and immersed myself in the cold running water.

It was in that river that I was to have the most consummate experience of my life. There were fish in the river, I knew; from time to time you could see the glint of their bodies flashing through the water. One summer morning I fell asleep with the stream rippling over me. How long I was asleep I don't know, but I was dreaming about the town of my childhood, Honfleur. I had gone back there as an old man and was walking the streets, stooped as ever, avoiding eye contact with passers-by. The women stared at me. Everything was as it always had been. I was old, but the market women had not aged at all. I made my way slowly down to the harbour. Bou-Bou, my mother, was standing by a fish stall with her back to me. I went towards her, whispering her name, but she didn't hear me. Before I reached her, she turned round and saw me. But I obviously made no impression on her whatsoever. She seemed not to recognize me. After looking straight at me for a moment, she walked off.

I was woken by a violent jerk of my body. An ice-cold shudder went through me and left me gasping for breath. I screamed. Looking down I saw a fish disappear between my legs. Hallelujah! Bliss! I had felt pain.

I had read about electric fish, though I couldn't remember where. Then slowly I began to realize that I had chanced upon something sensational. I sat in the gardener's cottage and stared at my notebooks: could it be electricity running through the nerve fibres? Could it be that pain arises when the electrical current is broken or meets another current? Had I been born with a weaker current than other people and was that why I had never been able to feel pain?

That night just before I fell asleep a little spasm went through my body. A tiny pain. Like a caress. Was the brain an electric machine? Was that spasm a sign that it was switching itself off for the night?

I went and lay down in the river again to wait for the fish. I lay there waiting every morning. Lying there was so good for reflective thought. Three months later I had another electric shock.

Pain is electrical!

*

In the summer of 1788 most of the country was hit by a devastating storm. Hailstones the size of rocks killed cats and hares and stripped fruit trees of their branches. Vineyards were wiped out, cornfields flattened, the hail pierced apples in Calvados and withered the olives and oranges in the Midi. Drought followed, and then the severest winter for eighty years. Bread became a luxury, with the price of a loaf rising to twelve *sous*. Laws were passed to prohibit bakers from charging more than fourteen and a half *sous*.

People bartered shirts for bread, and in one case a woman was known to have taken off her corset and given it to the baker in exchange for a loaf. The streets were full of hunger and violence. There were outbreaks of civil disorder.

The Mother Superior's carriage was attacked by a group of destitute peasants one Sunday morning on its way to Paris. Rumours of disturbances and months of starvation had caused a vicious hatred to erupt. As the sun broke through the clouds and shone in the window on to the Mother Superior's brow, they came rushing up out of the ditch, pulled the doors off their hinges and kicked the horses. They stripped the Mother Superior of her habit and robbed her of her box of money for new bibles. When she protested, in her gentle but slightly maternal and condescending tone, one of the women kicked her in the stomach. They took the coachman's new plumed hat, which upset him not a little. The horses were so frightened that they had to be led by the halter all the way back to the convent.

Inspector Ramon arrived at Sainte-Aure early the next morning. He was now the oldest inspector in the police force and was aware of being regarded as something of a curiosity. But it didn't trouble him. He had ceased caring what others thought a long time ago. He walked serenely along the path that wound its way between the convent's kitchen garden and the trim lawn with its hollyhocks planted in the English style. There was a black-clad figure on his knees weeding the garden. Out of habit, Ramon felt he should stop and take a look at him, even though he had had comments lately from his superiors about his time-wasting. Attention to detail was apparently no longer in fashion. Ramon called out a friendly question to the old man. As the latter turned the sunlight fell on his features. He was slight and rather stooped. Seeing the Inspector, he flinched, which took Ramon by surprise. Did it mean he recognized him? The man lowered his head again. Ramon went closer.

'Excuse me . . .'

The man looked up, somewhat reluctantly. Another grimace crossed his wizened little face. He obviously didn't like being spoken to and had no wish to converse, which aroused Ramon's suspicions. The man stood up slowly, his sharp eyes appraising Ramon. His mouth opened unnaturally wide when he spoke.

'Monsieur?'

Immediately, Ramon had a feeling he had heard that unusual voice before. He tried to remember where he might have seen the ugly visage. He held his hand up against the sun and squinted at him. He decided to adopt a jovial tone.

'I think I recall you from a previous case,' he said. 'It must have been some years ago, and I can't remember which one. Most annoying. My memory isn't what it was.'

The man gave a wan smile.

'You must be mistaken. I've never had anything to do with the police.'

Ramon gave him a quizzical look. He didn't like his defensiveness. Then he noticed the man's teeth: there was a half-moon-shaped piece missing from his left front tooth.

'Oh?'

For a moment Ramon had some difficulty recollecting, then suddenly it all fell into place. He was convinced that the piece of tooth he had found years before by the body of the Benedictine monk, Father Norcuill, would fit this fellow's jaw. He knew, without a doubt, that at last after all these years he had found the murderer. The rumours of his death must have been wrong. This must be Latour-Martin Quiros.

'I don't usually make mistakes. What's your name?'

A brief hesitation.

'Carteron.'

Ramon turned towards the convent building as if to break off the conversation and muttered the name he had been given. He shielded his eyes from the sun again. He was afraid, so afraid that he felt faint. He ought to push the old man to the ground and get the handcuffs on him, knock him out. But he didn't dare.

Why not?

Time had caught up with him. He had spent much of his life speculating about who the 'Anatomist' could have been. As he stood before him now, the man seemed simply too inadequate. He was an utter disappointment in comparison to the crimes committed. He looked a miserable wretch. It vexed Ramon, because it meant he had been on the wrong track for all those years and should have conducted his investigations completely differently.

'Can you show me the way in?' he finally asked. 'There are a few questions I want to ask about the attack on the Mother Superior's carriage last week. You probably heard about it.'

The man nodded. Ramon noticed that a smile crossed his lips, as if he guessed what was going on in the Inspector's mind and was secretly triumphant at his uncertainty.

'There was just one thing,' Ramon went on as they walked slowly through the garden towards the entrance to the building. The old man was limping. Ramon cleared his throat.

'May I ask you a question?'

The man nodded, a little surprised.

'This might be illogical,' he said tentatively, 'but do you ever find pieces of grit in cabbage? I lost half a tooth a few weeks ago when I was eating cabbage . . . Could it have anything to do with the way they are cropped, or am I jumping to the wrong conclusion? Have you ever had that problem?'

The man looked at Ramon expressionlessly and shook his head. Then he indicated the way to the Mother Superior's office and turned and hurried off as fast as he could to his gardener's cottage.

The Inspector went up the steps and into the cloisters. His shoes made much too loud an echo, he thought. He focussed on a point at the end of the colonnade and felt there was nothing that could prevent his legs from taking him there. Even if he decided to stop, his legs would go on walking and take him relentlessly along and through the door to the Mother Superior's office and thus give the murderer the chance to escape. He tried to find excuses. He couldn't arrest the man now. He would have to go back to the station first and try to find the fragment of tooth . . . His legs continued advancing automatically. He closed his eyes as he walked. He could hear the thudding of his heart. I'm afraid, he thought, and came to a standstill. Then he swung round and started retracing his route through the cloisters, his eyes still closed.

He clenched his fists as he walked and could taste the anger in his mouth. He opened his eyes again when he knew he had reached the steps, and ran down them and across the garden towards the little cottage.

He wrenched open the door, looked round, and caught his breath. The house was empty. He peered from corner to corner, as if expecting someone to be hiding in the shadows. There was no one there. He sat down on the doorstep and put his head on his knees. The man had gone. Ramon's mind emptied: for once all he could hear was silence. He went slowly over to the simple table in the middle of the room. On it was a gull, standing absolutely still on a wooden base and looking at him with fixed gaze. He had never seen a stuffed bird before, and was momentarily impressed by its lifelike appearance. He bent forward and picked it up, staring into lifeless eyes. The old seagull had its wings outstretched, as if it were about to fly away.

*

I was walking by the Seine, past the stone statues, the bridges, in a world of stone, head bent, the sound of people all around me. I kept looking over my shoulder. The noise of an excited crowd. Shots and cries. I couldn't see my pursuers, but I knew they were there. They had scissors and hammers in their hands and knew who I was. I caught sight of them at the corner of the Rue de Seine, a furious mob. Waving flags and axes aloft. A head on a stake. Blood in the streets. They had divided the city up between them. What was going on? Why such fury? Where would it lead? Where were they going?

I didn't understand.

They came streaming down the street, passing me as if they couldn't see me. They left a woman lying in the mud, dressed like an aristocrat but with her clothes hanging from her body in tatters. She had a slash down from her ear across to her breastbone. Her lace collar was crimson with blood. I stopped, wondering whether to approach her. Was she dead? No, she was groaning. It was hard to breathe — what had happened to the air in Paris? I wanted to turn away, but the sounds of the dying woman held me there. I knew I had to go over to her. I was afraid. I knelt down beside her. She had green eyes. She was sobbing. I stroked her cheek, knowing as I performed the useless gesture that I would do her no harm; I could feel her pain deep inside my own body, and began to weep. Then she went completely quiet.

I looked up. There were people at every window. What were they watching? Were they watching me? I could hear cannon fire in the distance. Smoke was billowing across the rooftops. Torn pages of books and shreds of clothing in the streets. I rose and hastened down to the banks of the river as quickly as I could, glimpsing some boats as I turned into the Place de Grève. I hid under one of them and closed my eyes, listening for the voices of my pursuers. Waiting for the shout of 'There he is!' and hands grabbing me.

But nothing happened. The hubbub continued and seemed as if it would never cease.

I didn't dare emerge before nightfall. I walked along past all the sinister façades and had no idea where to go.

I looked down at my legs. The sounds of shots and cannon fire were coming closer. I knew I had to run. I started running. I ran along the bank of the Seine. I looked down at my legs. Never in all my life had I run so fast. My feet were scarcely touching the ground. I was rising. I was flying up over the roof tops. I was leaving the smoking city. I was filled with pleasure and pain. I was Latour, and no one could catch me.

7

EPILOGUE
Charenton

In the winter of 1804 an emaciated old man arrived at the mental asylum of Charenton and handed a note to the porter in which he asked to see the Director, Monsieur Coulmier. He had to sit waiting for a long time outside the Director's office, and the porter was struck by his expression of despair. When he was finally admitted he gave Coulmier another piece of paper explaining that he was a man of science who wished to withdraw from the turmoil of the world to write his memoirs. This request was followed by a summary of his achievements. Coulmier looked up from his desk at the stooped figure in front of him. He seemed more dejected than proud, and was obviously not concerned about the Director's opinion of his curriculum vitæ. Anatomy of the brain. Discoverer of the human electrical system. Had also identified the 'pain centre' of the body. Coulmier's first impression was that he had before him a deeply disturbed human being. Latour uttered not a single word during their meeting, to all appearances dumb. When Coulmier told him that in the normal course of events they had no rooms for scientists, but that in his case they would give the matter their consideration, Latour smiled. He wrote that he was willing to pay for his board and lodging.

The doctors examined him and declared him to have been born an idiot and never to have spoken, though there was nothing physically wrong with his speech organs. He was undernourished and had a disposition to melancholy and obsessiveness. Coulmier called him in again and was pleased to be able to say that they could find him a place in the new wing. He would be patient number 423. Seeing a joyless smile cross his sorrowful countenance, Coulmier went on to explain that he would not be allowed to conduct scientific experiments in the hospital. Latour, who had listened in silence, suddenly leant across the table, seized pen and paper and wrote with agitated hand, 'I have come to write my memoirs'. Coulmier read the sentence. He was about to explain to him again that he could not let him pursue scientific studies at Charenton, but when he looked into Latour's azure blue eyes he had a feeling that he might be on the track of something interesting and that any rules might hinder him from making new discoveries. This strange man fascinated him, so he decided to encourage his writing. He would keep an eye on him. He tried to get him to say his name, but he apparently could not remember. 'Don't know,' was what he wrote on the paper. So at Charenton he was given the nickname Don't-Know.

Only a few years earlier the asylum had been in a neglected state. The buildings were falling into disrepair, the trees in the garden had been uprooted to bring in 264 francs, and there were only sixteen beds left. The new Director had renovated everything, added a women's wing, and within those few years the asylum had been able to take in several hundred patients.

Coulmier was inspired by the theories of the great philanthropist Pinel. The patients were divided according to diagnosis: hypochondria, melancholia, lunacy, mania, idiocy. Unruly and dangerous patients were kept isolated in separate wards. 'The best treatment for strong passions is time and patience,' he used to say. For those who knew him, the Director's words sounded like a prescription that could apply to himself. He was a very energetic man whose thought processes advanced by leaps and bounds. The asylum was an open institution for the insane. They had to be brought out of their dark prisons into the airy gardens of liberty and responsibility. Coulmier did not believe in chains and whips as a method of treatment. He was certain that beneath the violence of madness there lay a disturbed and despondent mind, that the sick should be listened to, that some logic could be discerned in their confused utterances, clear images extracted from their dreams. The insane could be made to recognize the futility of their madness and to condemn their own behaviour through remorse and self-reproach and thus re-establish reason in their brains. Patients had to be weaned away from the chaos of irrationality and gradually made to comply with the laws and morality of society.

'Insanity is simply insanity.'

People spoke of Coulmier's 'moral method', though no one seemed entirely sure of its meaning.

Coulmier soon became aware of certain oddities in the behaviour of his 'man of science'. He wandered about the asylum as if cut off from the world of others by an insuperable barrier. Yet he seemed to be torturing himself by constantly seeking to discover the cause of his own isolation. He would stand in the background listening, alternately hiding and creeping closer. But never going right up to the others.

A year earlier, in April 1803, the writer and former revolutionary D.A.F. de Sade had been transferred from Bicêtre Asylum to Charenton. De Sade had made a name for himself during and after the Revolution, a free spirit, a banned writer, and had been fêted as a hero until as an officially appointed member of the jury he had started to oppose the death penalty, not least in the case against his parents-in-law. He was outlawed from society and lived a life of poverty with a woman he called 'Sensitivity', until in 1801 he was suspected of having written a pamphlet against the Emperor entitled *Zoloé*.

Coulmier immediately noticed the 'scientist's' special interest in De Sade, even though the two men never exchanged a word nor gave any sign of mutual recognition. The dumb man's eyes positively lit up when the police searched De Sade's cell for manuscripts or any strange devices for masturbation. He would often be lurking in the distance when De Sade strode through the asylum venting his tyrannical depression on everyone, shouting at the staff and embracing melancholics, or putting his lips to the Director's ear to whisper coarse words in ingratiating tones.

Coulmier and De Sade shared an appetite for the philosophy of the flesh, libertinism. There were many who were of the opinion that they were both equally unappetising characters. Coulmier vehemently asserted that it was an insult to the asylum and to the personal integrity of the Director that people like Désorgues the poet and De Sade were sent to Charenton accused of publishing derogatory writings about Napoleon. They were Coulmier's 'political patients', and he did not like the premise. The logic was too simplistic: if you did not admire the Emperor you must be mad. But De Sade was to play a significant role in Coulmier's development of treatment methods at Charenton, even if his contribution was never acknowledged. At De Sade's suggestion Coulmier had a theatre built above the women's wing, with seating for over two hundred spectators. Theatre productions were part of Coulmier's 'moral treatment', and De Sade himself was play-wright, instructor, organizer, actor and the asylum's suave host after the performances. The productions were directed by De Sade and performed by the inmates, with a few individual actors brought in from the Opera. Well-known characters were given original interpretations. On one occasion De Sade put a live chimpanzee on stage, to the great glee of audience and patients alike. The productions eventually achieved enormous popularity in sophisticated Parisian circles, and Charenton became a place of pilgrimage to see De Sade's 'crazy productions'. Coulmier's view was that they diverted the patients and alleviated their melancholia.

Latour never went to a performance. When the fashionable élite came down from Paris to see the infamous De Sade and his disciples, Latour took flight as far from all the commotion as he could get. Coulmier still had a feeling that De Sade and the 'scientist' knew one another, even though they never spoke and were never seen together. There was something about the way the dumb man followed De Sade around that bore witness to a deeper and perhaps fraught relationship.

Coulmier's suspicions continued to nag at him, so he decided to try to find out more. He encouraged Latour to write his memoirs. They would be of great interest for future generations, he said. He then ensured that Latour's room was inspected regularly. He discovered his name and he read his notes, building up a picture of all that had happened as the writing progressed.

He read that Latour had been a pupil of Rouchefoucault and the valet of De Sade. There were constant references to experiments, and to cadavers. And to some kind of contract, a list he felt compelled to work his way through. Latour was clearly trying to ascribe some meaning to his experiences, but Coulmier was sure of one thing: there was no meaning to be found in violence. It was obvious that there was one episode that had affected Latour deeply, that seemed to bind him and De Sade together and yet also to hold them apart. In Savoy, on the run from the law, De Sade had witnessed one of Latour's criminal acts. When Latour wrote about it, De Sade's watchful eyes seemed to take on a symbolic significance for him. It was no longer just his master's eyes, it was everyone's eyes upon him, God's eyes, and not least the victims' eyes. Latour had felt pain for the first time only in old age, and that pain had become a bridge to the pain of others. Coulmier concluded that it was sympathy, not cruelty, that had led to Latour's mental illness. The more he wrote, the more muddled his explanation of events became. He went over the same problems again and again, never finding his way out. At length the relationship to the Marquis changed in the text itself: where before he had been spoken of with respect, even with affection, he now became the cause of everything that had gone wrong. Latour's mention of a catalogue, a list of names, had an ominous ring. Coulmier had the impression that Latour was suffering from a compulsive urge to circle closer and closer round De Sade. He was now having fantasies of cutting him up.

It was some time before the Director came to believe that Latour actually did have designs on De Sade's life. But even when he saw increasing evidence of this possibility in Latour's notes, he did nothing to alert De Sade. Partly because he felt sure that De Sade was aware of the danger himself, and partly because his interest in Latour's development was greater than his interest in De Sade's fragile health. More and more sinister hints kept cropping up in Latour's narrative, almost as if he knew that Coulmier was reading it and was indirectly explaining his motives and warning him. When Coulmier became convinced that Latour really had murdered several people in Paris he put a junior attendant to watch him round the clock and give him a detailed account of Latour's movements.

He read Latour's notes even more carefully from then on, trying to analyse the mind of a murderer. A Sadian mentality, developed under the influence of the divine Marquis. There was an interesting personality trait in these two men, an inclination to obsession and arrogance, a combination of rationality and madness that turned the one into a murderer and the other into a dramatist. Coulmier was convinced that this might be significant scientific material and that in some ways it was symptomatic of the times they lived in. When he had solved the puzzle he would write a little treatise on it. After that he would hand over Latour's notes to the police and make sure that he was tried and executed.

When Latour suddenly stopped writing, Coulmier seriously considered discharging him. He didn't trust him and was afraid of what he might get up to. This 'man of science' was obviously going through a crisis: he burnt his confessions and lay motionless in his room, as if in a trance. It was curiosity that induced Coulmier to let him remain in the asylum, and after a while he took up his pen again. There was an apparent clarity in what he was writing now, which surprised Coulmier. He described daily life in the asylum so minutely that the Director really began to fear for De Sade's life. Why otherwise should he record the times of the changes of shift in De Sade's wing? Yet Coulmier knew he had nothing more than assumptions to go on; in all the abstracts he had made from Latour's notebooks there was not a single sentence that could serve as definite proof of anything.

Latour managed to climb out of the window unobserved. He was dressed in nothing but a cloak and a thin pair of shoes. It was winter, with frost still on the ground. As he walked the length of the west wing he knew he was getting old. He had to take small paces, his knees creaked, he felt tottery. He stopped and looked at the scalpel in his hand. He put it between his teeth and clambered up the sturdy ivy towards De Sade's room. His back and his arm ached with the effort of hauling himself up. The window was closed and he had to force it. Only by using all his strength did he eventually succeed in prising it open and slipping inside. He took the scalpel out of his mouth and went over to the bed. There appeared to be a figure huddled up under the bedclothes. The word freedom came into his mind. But as he raised the scalpel to slice into the covers he heard a sound behind him. He spun round quickly and peered into the darkness. There in the corner sat the Marquis, his arms folded across his chest.

The next morning De Sade was seen going into Latour's room with a piece of paper in his hand. Seconds later he emerged empty-handed. Coulmier had the room searched, but nothing was found. Latour was allowed to return to his room after three weeks in solitary confinement. He immediately became calmer and more passive. All signs of murder plans and persecution complexes disappeared from his writing. Instead he seemed to withdraw into himself, and spent most of the time sitting motionless in his room. He did not mingle with the other patients at all, and had no more than an amiable and compliant nod for the doctors. Coulmier gave him up as an incurable case. An unfathomable mind.

In the autumn of 1814 De Sade fell ill. He was afflicted with severe pains in the lower part of his stomach and in his testicles, and was put on a diet. The doctors forbade him to drink wine. His sexual organs were very sore, especially when he touched them at night, and in the end he asked the doctors to fit a suspensorium. Towards the end of November his condition deteriorated to such an extent that he could no longer walk. He had attacks of gangrenous fever. On 30th November he wrote in his diary: 'They have put a truss on me for the first time.' Those words were the last he wrote. On Friday 2nd December he developed breathing problems and died.

He left a comprehensive will, and was especially punctilious about the disposal of his corpse. He absolutely forbade the opening of his body. He wished to be transported in a simple wooden coffin to his lands at Malmaison, near Epernon. He wanted to be laid to rest, without any kind of ceremony, in the first coppice on the right. The grave was to be dug by the tenant farmer of Malmaison, under the supervision of Monsieur Le Normand, timber merchant. The latter could, if he so desired, invite those of De Sade's relatives who, with no kind of funeral trappings whatsoever, wished to accord him that last token of affection. Once the grave was covered, it should be sown with acorns, so that trees would grow and erase every sign of his grave from the face of the earth, '. . . in the same way that my memory shall be erased from the minds of men, with the exception of the few who loved me to the last and whose tender memory I bear with me to the grave'.

But these wishes were not carried out. De Sade's resting place was dug up. A young doctor from Charenton asked for De Sade's skull and was given it. He had it examined by the German anatomist Dr Spurtzheim, a pioneer of what was called phrenology. Dr Spurtzheim concluded his investigation with the assertion that De Sade's bizarre personality was attributable to the over-development of certain organs of the brain.

Some weeks afterwards Latour also fell ill. Coulmier had him moved to another room, and during the cleaning of his old room they found a poem hidden under the mattress. Coulmier recognized the writing immediately as De Sade's. The paper was very crumpled; the Director stood with it in his hands thinking of the lengths Latour must have gone to in keeping it concealed for so long. The handwriting was difficult to decipher, but he knew it must be the paper De Sade had placed in Latour's room after the murder attempt. This was the poem that had made Latour change his mind about fulfilling his plan and killing De Sade. The Director read these lines:

237

Epitaph on D.A.F. Sade
Prisoner Under All Regimes
By Himself

Passers-by,
Kneel here and pray
By the grave of an unhappy man.
In the last century he was born,
Of insult and injury he died.
The tyranny of evil men
Broke his spirit and crushed him.
Under an Absolute Monarchy
He was fettered by a monster.
Under the Terror the pain continued,
Pushing him relentlessly towards Hell.
The time of the Consulate offered no respite:
The sacrifice was again De Sade.

Coulmier closed his eyes in sorrow. He felt cheated. He had failed. The career of a murderer had been brought to an end by a sheet of paper, a sheet of paper with twelve lines of verse on it, instead of by the great Coulmier. He put the poem back where it had been found and returned to his office. That night he pondered ways of ridding himself of Latour. But regretted it the next day, when as so often the morning brought a pang of conscience. He decided that the old valet should be allowed to see out his days at Charenton, as his master had.

*

How did I come to end up here, in this room where I'm always freezing cold?

Why won't they stop watching me, with their vigilant eyes? As if I have to be examined again and again, investigated, dissected. Latour-Martin Quiros shall not be left in peace. What do they think of me? What words are they using? Words they have always used about me?

I feel naked. I am too old. I spend most of my time asleep. I try to think about myself as I doze, about who I was. But my thoughts have no substance. There is no meaning in anything any more. I have only one fantasy left. I cut open the Marquis' skull, but do not find what I have been seeking. The fantasy recurs again and again; it is all I have. Then I wake up and weep because the old aristocrat is no more.

My intentions of becoming a great scientist were ludicrous, but I am not inclined to laugh. There is too much emptiness in me for that.

I feel naked. Too old. I have reached an exorbitant age. I never wanted to live so long.

Coulmier, the Director, comes to see me from time to time. His eyes are so penetrating that they hurt. He asks questions, even though he knows he will never get any answers. I think he knows more about me than he should, and much more than I would like. He asks me about Honfleur, about my mother. He asks about Paris and the old Marquis. I stare at him in silence. Motionless. Silence is the only power I have.